NICK AND TESLA'S

SPECIAL EFFECTS
SPECTACULAR

ALSO AVAILABLE:

Nick and Tesla's
High-Voltage Danger Lab

Nick and Tesla's
Robot Army Rampage

Nick and Tesla's
Secret Agent Gadget Battle

Nick and Tesla's
Super-Cyborg Gadget Glove

NICK AND TESLA'S

SPECIAL EFFECTS SPECTACULAR

A MYSTERY WITH
**ANIMATRONICS, ALIEN MAKEUP,
CAMERA GEAR, AND
OTHER MOVIE MAGIC YOU
CAN MAKE YOURSELF**

BY "SCIENCE BOB"
PFLUGFELDER
AND STEVE
HOCKENSMITH

ILLUSTRATIONS BY
SCOTT GARRETT

QUIRK BOOKS
PHILADELPHIA

Copyright © 2015 by Quirk Productions, Inc.

All rights reserved. No part of this book may be reproduced in any form without written permission from the publisher.

Library of Congress Cataloging in Publication Number: 2014944416

ISBN: 978-1-59474-760-1

Printed in the United States of America
Typeset in Caecilia, Futura, and Russell Square

Designed by Andie Reid, based on a design by Doogie Horner
Illustrations by Scott Garrett
Production management by John J. McGurk

Quirk Books
215 Church Street
Philadelphia, PA 19106
quirkbooks.com

10 9 8 7 6 5 4 3 2 1

DANGER! DANGER! DANGER! DANGER!

The how-to projects in this book involve hot water, projectiles, hot glue, and other potentially dangerous elements. Before you build any of the projects, ASK AN ADULT TO REVIEW THE INSTRUCTIONS. You'll probably need their help with one or two of the steps, anyway.

Although we believe these projects to be safe and family-friendly, accidents can happen in any situation; we cannot guarantee your safety. THE AUTHORS AND PUBLISHER DISCLAIM ANY LIABILITY FROM ANY HARM OR INJURY THAT MAY RESULT FROM THE USE, PROPER OR IMPROPER, OF THE INFORMATION CONTAINED IN THIS BOOK. Remember, the instructions in this book are not meant to be a substitute for your good judgment and common sense.

There was a muffled boom, and then the whole house seemed to rise about half an inch before slamming down again. The lights flickered but stayed on.

Nick and Tesla Holt listened intently. After a moment, they could hear faint coughing coming from downstairs.

"I'm all right!" their uncle said from the basement. "You don't have to call the fire department this time!" Uncle Newt was an inventor and a scientist, and he'd recently set aside his favorite project—a compost-powered vacuum cleaner—to begin work on something that he wouldn't tell his niece and nephew about. "It's a surprise!" Uncle Newt shouted, coughing a bit more. That was all he ever said about his new endeavor, no matter how many times Nick and Tesla asked him about it.

"It would really be a surprise," Nick said to his sister, "if his 'whatever-it-is' didn't blow up all the time."

"He could be tinkering with a new flavor of ice cream, and there'd be a 99 percent chance it would go up in flames," Tesla said to her twin brother. They'd known their uncle only since the beginning of the summer, when they'd been sent to stay with him in Half Moon Bay while their parents traveled abroad. But they'd soon realized that anything their inventor uncle happened to be working on was prone to exploding.

Nick was sitting on the floor of the bedroom he and Tesla shared, hunched over a battered but functional laptop (which they also shared). He shrugged at Tesla and then looked down again at the computer. When he clicked the mouse, a black-and-white image of a man with dark hair and a thick mustache, dressed in old-fashioned clothes, appeared on the screen. Tesla recognized the man instantly.

It was Tesla. *Nikola* Tesla, that is. The brilliant, eccentric inventor after whom she and Nick ("Nikola," according to his birth certificate) had been named by their parents. (Who were also scientists but, unlike Uncle Newt, had never blown anything up. At least as far as Nick and Tesla knew.)

Nick scrolled down and another image slid into place: a long, single-story brick building with, looming over it, a tower topped by a huge, bulbous dome.

Tesla recognized this picture, too. It showed Wardenclyffe Tower, which was sometimes called Tesla Tower. Nikola Tesla had built it over a century ago. It was supposed to transmit electric power through the air like radio signals . . . except it had never worked properly.

Nick had been obsessively researching wireless power transmission for days. He was convinced it had something to do with their mom and dad's disappearance. Supposedly their parents had left the twins with Uncle Newt so that they could fly to Uzbekistan to research soybean irrigation. Yet they had been out of touch ever since, and Nick and Tesla eventually found themselves being shadowed by spies and government agents. It was one of those agents who'd suggested that wireless energy transfer, the kind that Nikola Tesla tried to invent, had something to do with their parents' vanishing.

"You know," Nick said, without looking up from the laptop, "someone with a real, working Tesla Tower could put every oil and gas company out of business overnight. Maybe that's why it has to be such a big secret."

"And someone with a real, working magic wand could turn the Great Lakes into chocolate syrup and put Hershey's out of business, but that doesn't mean it's going to happen," Tesla answered.

"Yeah, well, we're a lot closer to having wireless power transmission than we are to magic wands." Now that he was getting excited, Nick looked up at his sister to continue the debate. "That solar power company Solanow has a prototype energy emitter, right?[1] And the Japanese government wants to build a network of space-based solar power transmitters.[2] And—"

---

1   They found out this information in their earlier mystery, *Nick and Tesla's Super-Cyborg Gadget Glove.*—The authors

2   This information wasn't in *Nick and Tesla's Super-Cyborg Gadget Glove.* It's just true.—The authors

"I'm just glad Uncle Newt's not working on wireless power transmission," Tesla said, interrupting her brother. "If he were, every electrical appliance on the West Coast would've exploded already."

"Ha," Nick said mirthlessly, and then he went back to staring at the computer screen.

"Hey," Tesla said, trying not to sound like she'd been planning to ask this question the whole time, "why don't you take a break and come help me? I need to build a stabilizer for Silas's video camera. Something that'll help him get cool, smooth shots. He's at DeMarco's house right now filming his superhero movie. You know, *Bald Eagle: The Legend Takes Flight*. You should see DeMarco's little sister Elesha in that green alien makeup we made for them."

Tesla was talking about Silas Kuskie and DeMarco Davison, the only friends she and her brother had made (so far) during their stay in Half Moon Bay. Nick believed that no *normal* kids would want the kind of trouble that he and his sister tended to get into. But DeMarco was an adrenaline junkie, always up for something exciting and a little dangerous. And Silas . . . well, let's just say that thinking ahead about the kind of trouble he might get into—or thinking ahead about anything, for that matter—just wasn't his style.

Nick didn't even look up as his sister continued her pitch.

"Silas shot some footage of their stunt dummy dressed as the Bald Eagle, and the video was so jumpy and jerky that just watching it made Monique"—Monique was DeMarco's even littler sister—"puke all over the yard."

Nick kept typing. Tesla frowned. She was sure Nick would enjoy the idea of one of DeMarco's nasty little sisters getting so sick that she vomited. The two girls had been tormenting DeMarco ever since they were old enough to throw things at his head.

"So, Silas needs something like a Steadicam," Tesla continued. "You've seen those, right?"

Nick still didn't respond.

"It's a frame that spreads out a movie camera's center of gravity via a counterbalance, making it easy to smoothly manipulate the camera with a special kind of joint called a gimbal." Tesla kept talking even though Nick continued to ignore her. "Like the ones gyroscopes have. So, your video camera stays level instead of bouncing and jerking around and you get nice, even shots."

"I know what a Steadicam is," Nick answered.

"Well, we can't make the real thing, of course. But I have some ideas for a simpler version that would work with that little video camera Silas uses." Then Tesla had an idea. "We'll call it a Silascam," she said. "No, a Teslacam. No, wait—a Nickandteslacam. It could probably work with a phone camera, too."

"Great. Go make it without me."

"I can, of course. But it'd be a lot easier *with* you." Usually, Nick and Tesla built all kinds of things together: vinegar and liquid-soap "volcanoes," homemade rock candy, robots, super-cyborg gadget gloves. Last week, they'd created an animatronic arm, mostly out of ice-pop sticks, which Silas used in his movie along with the alien makeup. They'd also helped Silas and DeMarco put together a stunt dummy for the action scenes (even stuntman-wannabe DeMarco had no interest in falling down a flight of stairs, jumping from an attic window, or doing any of the other crazy tricks Silas came up with). Tesla tried to distract herself from all the weirdness and worries about their parents by keeping busy with one project after another. Lately, however, Nick hadn't been trying to distract himself from those concerns. On the contrary: he'd been wallowing in them, trying to find an answer by scouring the Internet for clues.

And now Tesla wanted to build something, anything, with her brother.

Nick clicked on a link, and a new webpage opened on-screen. The title was "The SHOCKING Truth behind Tesla's Death Ray."

"Sorry," Nick said. "I'm busy."

"No," Tesla said, "you're obsessed."

Nick didn't respond. So Tesla decided it was time to play dirty.

"You know, I found something really interesting online last night," Tesla said. "Here, let me show you."

She plopped down next to her brother and shouldered him away from the keyboard.

"Hey!" he said in protest.

"This'll just take a sec. Trust me, you're going to be amazed."

Tesla opened a folder on the desktop, found the icon she was looking for—a tiny traffic signal—and double-clicked it.

"There," she said. "Done."

Nick squinted at the screen.

"Nothing's happening," he said.

"Exactly. I just turned on Stoplite."

"What's Stoplite?"

"A program that automatically freezes your computer for six hours, so you won't waste your whole day on it."

"*What?*" Nick shoved his sister aside and began jabbing at the keyboard. The screen remained frozen.

"I'll just restart it," he said.

He held down the power button but . . . nothing happened.

"Stoplite's really good," Tesla said.

"Oh, man! This is *not* funny, Tez!"

"It's not supposed to be funny. It's supposed to get you off your butt so you'll come downstairs and help me."

"Oh, yeah, right. Like I'm going to help you after you did *this*."

Nick folded his arms across his chest and stared at the wall.

"Suit yourself," Tesla said. "I'm going down to the lab to get the parts. If Silas never finishes his cinematic masterpiece and doesn't become the world's greatest twelve-year-old film director, it won't be my fault."

She got up and headed for the door.

Nick stayed put.

"Well, good luck building your little whatever," he said with a growl. "Because you won't be getting any help from me."

WITHDRAWN

Uncle Newt let Tesla stay in the basement laboratory just long enough to gather the materials and tools she needed.

"Shoo! Out!" he said, flapping his hands at her when she'd collected an armful of PVC tubing.

"It smells weird down here. Like . . . the air after a thunderstorm," Tesla said.

"Go! Top secret!" said Uncle Newt, still flapping.

"And what happened to you?"

Uncle Newt's long, unkempt gray-blond hair was standing up so straight that the ends were brushing the rafters overhead.

"Vamoose! Scram!" he said.

"Okay, okay, I'm going. Geez."

Tesla stomped up the stairs and through the kitchen to the dining room.

Nick was sitting there waiting for her.

"All right," he said with a sigh. "What are we making again?"

"I don't think you appreciate the *gravity* of your situation, Bald Eagle!" Lady Evilika said, cackling. The scaly green alien pointed her power scepter at the feather-covered superhero standing stiffly on the tree branch above her. "Mega-mass blast!"

Bald Eagle toppled over and plummeted to earth, his crimson cape flapping the whole way down. He landed headfirst, yet he didn't crumple. Instead, his body slammed backward against the tree trunk and remained absolutely rigid, with his helmeted head on the ground and the soles of his white boots facing the sky.

Bald Eagle was standing on his head.

"Cut!" yelled the director, a.k.a. Silas Kuskie. Which was completely unnecessary—Silas was also the cameraman, so he was only yelling at himself.

Silas switched off the camera and stalked toward the fallen hero—which was really just a newspaper-stuffed stunt dummy, still leaning against the tree from which it had fallen.

"You can't just push Michael over!" Silas shouted to a small, wiry, twelve-year-old boy perched precariously on a branch. ("Michael" was what Silas called the stunt dummy, by the way. He'd named it after one of his least-favorite film directors.) "You've got to *throw* him," he added, "really give him some lift!

Bald Eagle's trying to fly away, and you're making it look like he just fell asleep!"

"How can I throw the dummy when I need to keep one hand on the tree, so I don't fall out?" asked the boy in the tree, a.k.a. DeMarco.

"How should I know?" Silas answered. "You're the stunt coordinator! So coordinate it!"

Nick and Tesla arrived, carrying their just-completed Silascam—which they secretly called a Nickandteslacam—as Silas was checking the fallen Michael for damage. "You guys overstuffed him," Silas said when he saw the two siblings approaching. "There's no give to the limbs. You need to take out some of the newspaper. Loosen him up a bit. Make him more lifelike." He turned the dummy right side up and leaned it against the tree. "All I want is perfection! Is that so much to ask?"

"Is he really turning into a perfectionist tyrant," Nick whispered as Silas went back to yelling instructions up at DeMarco, "or is he just acting that way because he thinks a movie director is *supposed* to be a perfectionist tyrant?"

Tesla shrugged. "Maybe both?" She held up the apparatus that she and Nick had created; it was a junction of PVC pipes that balanced on a screw-driver. "Here's your . . . uh . . . Silascam," she said.

Silas stared at the camera rig for a moment, blinking quickly.

"You attach your camera here, to this bolt . . ." Nick started to explain.

"It's . . . it's . . . beautiful," Silas murmured, taking the contraption from Tesla so carefully that she and Nick (and DeMarco, who had dropped out of the tree) could only watch in stunned silence. Silas never handled *anything* carefully, with the exception of his prized copy of *Metal Man #2*. "If this works," he continued, "I'll mention you guys in my Oscar acceptance speech."

"Umm, okay," Nick said.

"Okay, okay. Let's go, people!" Silas barked suddenly. "We're gonna set everything up and run it again. Places! Chop-chop!" And just like that, Silas the movie director was back.

Then Lady Evilika—who was in fact DeMarco's seven-year-old sister Elesha in green alien makeup and a "spacesuit" made of old footie pajamas and aluminum foil—came stalking toward her brother. "Tell me to 'chop-chop' again," she said with an om-

inous growl, "and I'll chop-chop *you*."

"Yeah, she'll chop-chop *you*," chimed in Elesha's "executive makeup and wardrobe assistant"—in other words, her little sister, Monique. Together, Elesha and Monique weighed nowhere near as much as tall, stocky Silas. But what they lacked in size, they more than made up for in aggression.

Silas looked at their scowling faces, formed a quivering smile, and then flapped a hand toward Nick, Tesla, and DeMarco.

"The chop-chop was for them," he explained. "You go back to your mark in your own time, Elesha."

Elesha's and Monique's eyes narrowed.

"Please," Silas added quickly.

Without another word, Elesha stalked off toward the spot where she'd started the scene. Her little sister tagged along, touching up Elesha's green makeup as she went.

"We warned you not to use my sisters in his movie," DeMarco said, keeping his voice low.

"Lady Evilika is an undead alien monster queen," Silas answered. "It's a role Elesha was born for!"

DeMarco and Tesla went to work trying to get Michael the nonhuman hero back up into the tree. The stunt dummy wasn't so heavy, being made mostly from electrical tape and scrunched-up newsprint. But the bulky bird costume it was wearing—a modified owl mascot suit given to the kids by a local museum—added another twenty pounds to its weight. DeMarco shimmied his way up to his spot on a low branch.

"Push harder!" DeMarco said, grunting down in Tesla's direction.

"Pull harder!" Tesla said, grunting back up at him.

"If you want something done right . . ." Silas said and groaned an exasperated groan. He set down his video camera, took the dummy in both hands, and heaved it up into the tree with such force that it nearly knocked DeMarco off his branch.

"I bet Cash Ashkinos doesn't have to throw stunt dummies into trees," Silas groused as he picked up the video camera again and got back into position to shoot the scene. "He's probably got, like, a dummy wrangler for that."

"Really?" Tesla asked, sarcastically. "And how many Cash Ashkinos movies have dummies in trees?"

"Three," answered Silas.

"Four," said DeMarco.

"*Three*," repeated Silas.

DeMarco shook his head.

"*Four.*"

Silas began counting them on his fingers. "*Troubleshooter 5. Crash Course 3. Morphbots 2.*"

"And *Street Race 6: Pedal to the Metal.*"

Silas furrowed his brow. "I don't remember a dummy in a tree in . . ." he muttered. "Ooooooh, yeah! When that one guy uses the ejector seat to squash that other guy against a giant redwood." Silas stared up at the dummy for a moment and then said, "He really knows how to use a stunt dummy. It's why he's my favorite director. I wonder which kind of tree Cash Ashkinos prefers to put stunt dummies in?"

"You can ask him yourself," DeMarco replied from his perch, "because we're going to meet him today."

Nick and Tesla exchanged the kind of look people give each other when they want to shake their heads and roll their eyes, but they don't want anyone to see.

"I saw that!" DeMarco yelled to them. "But believe me, we really *are* going to meet—"

"Action!" Silas shouted, and then Elesha began her speech. "I don't think you appreciate the *gravity* of your situation, Bald Eagle . . ."

SUPER-STABLE
CAMERA-STEADY RIG
(A.K.A. SILASCAM, A.K.A. NICKANDTESLACAM)

THE STUFF

- 1 piece of PVC pipe, 18 inches (46 cm) long (for this project, use pipe and connectors labeled ¾ inch wide; the opening should be just large enough for a penny to fit inside)

- 2 pieces of PVC pipe, each 7 inches (18 cm) long

- 2 pieces of PVC pipe, each 6 inches (15 cm) long

- 1 piece of PVC pipe, 1½ inches (4 cm) long

- 3 90-degree angle pieces

- 2 T-connectors

- 1 end cap

- 1 Phillips head screwdriver

- 1 kitchen sponge

- Tape

- Scissors

- Lots of pennies (you may want to get a few rolls at the bank

Continued on next page

FOR USE WITH A CAMERA PHONE:

- 2 clothespins

- 2 or more rubber bands

FOR USE WITH A LIGHTWEIGHT VIDEO CAMERA:

- ¼-inch bolt (or whichever size fits your camera's tripod mount) and nut

- Drill

1. Arrange the pipes and connectors as shown in the illustration. Push the pipes into the connectors until they fit tightly; if needed, use a hammer to tap the pipes together. If the fit seems too loose, secure them with glue (use a type made for plastics).

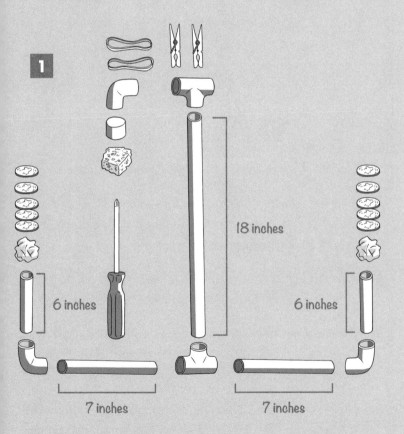

18 inches

6 inches

6 inches

7 inches

7 inches

NOTE: If you're going to use this stabilizer with a cell-phone camera, and you're planning to glue the pieces together, it will be a little easier to place the clothespins and rubber bands (Final Step 1) before you attach the 90-degree angle piece to the top T-connector.

2. Cut out a 1-inch-square (2.5 cm) piece of sponge.

3. Push the sponge into the end cap so that it fits snugly and doesn't fall out when the cap is turned upside down (if it falls out, cut a larger piece of sponge).

4. Tape the end cap, open side (with the sponge) out, to the open end of the 90-degree angle piece at the top of the rig.

5. Ball up some small pieces of paper or tissue; using a pencil or screwdriver, push them to the bottom of each of the 6-inch (15 cm) tubes.

6. Fill the back 7-inch pipe (the one on the same side as the 90-degree angle piece and end cap) with pennies all the

way to the top. Tape over the top of the pipe so that the pennies don't fall out.

7. Insert the head of the screwdriver into the center of the sponge, as shown, and hold the handle while allowing your camera steadier to hang freely. The sponge should keep the point of the screwdriver from slipping. Next, add pennies to the front pipe until the camera steadier hangs perfectly straight up and down. Tape the top of the pipe to keep the pennies in.

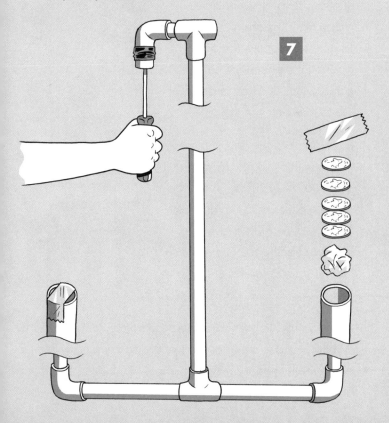

THE FINAL STEPS

1. For a smartphone camera,
    use rubber bands to attach a
    clothespin to either side of the
    top T-connector, as shown. The
    clips should hold the phone in
    place. (To protect your phone,
    you can use a screen protector
    or slip pieces of sponge be-
    tween the clips and the screen.)
    To get the smoothest images,
    position the phone so that the
    camera lens is as close as possi-
    ble to the center of the pipes.

    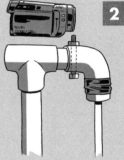

2. For a lightweight video camera
    with camera mount, ask an adult
    to drill a $5/16$-inch hole in the top
    angle piece. Use a nut and bolt
    (usually ¼ inch) to attach the
    camera. Secure the camera with
    the nut from below.

    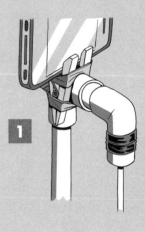

3. Now you're ready to look like a
    professional Hollywood camera operator! Remember: this
    stabilizer is designed for lightweight cameras. Just like the
    pros, you'll need to practice—experiment until you get the
    hang of it. Some tips:

- Take small, smooth steps as you move the camera.

- Avoid suddenly speeding up or slowing down.

- Your camera may sway as you move; use your free hand to gently guide or nudge it to face the desired direction.

- It's tempting to look at the screen, but keep your eyes on the front pipe of the camera rig. You'll be better able to judge if the steadier is, well, steady!

"Come over here and look at this," Silas said to Monique.

The younger girl was touching up her older sister's alien makeup while the rest of the crew—Silas, DeMarco, Tesla, and Nick—crowded around the camera.

"Why?" Monique asked, eyeing Silas suspiciously.

He gestured toward the camera's view screen. On it, Lady Evilika could be seen blasting the dummy Bald Eagle out of the tree. The scene played out in smooth, swooping shots, courtesy of the Silascam.

"I want to see if this scene makes you throw up, like the last time," Silas said.

Monique just glared at him a moment before returning to dab more green paint on Elesha's face.

"Don't worry," DeMarco said. "No one'll throw up looking at this."

"Yeah, you're right. It's perfect," Silas said. "It looks totally slick. Totally classy. Now, let's set up for the scene where Bald Eagle rips Lady Evilika's arms off."

"Totally classy," Nick muttered.

Silas overheard him. "Hey, it is!" he shot back defensively. "It's not like we're showing a *person* getting her arms ripped off. It's just her." He pointed at his sister.

"What did you say?" Elesha said.

She'd been sitting on the edge of a big sandbox in DeMarco's backyard, but now she rose and took a step toward Silas.

"An undead alien, I meant! Lady Evilika!" Silas said in a squeaky voice.

Elesha sat down again.

"Man," Silas said under his breath, "the movie business is *stressful*."

"If we're doing the arms sequence, we'll need to get the Bald Eagle costume off Michael so you can put it on," Tesla said. (Silas wasn't just the screenwriter, director, and executive producer of *Bald Eagle: The Legend Takes Flight*. He was also the star.)

"Right," Silas said. "You guys do that while I plan how I'm going to shoot this scene."

He picked up the notebook and pen he'd left next to a tree and wandered off toward the woods behind the Davisons' yard. "Now," he said, as if to himself, "how would Cash Ashkinos do this scene?"

Tesla and DeMarco walked over to the dummy lying facedown on the ground. Getting the figure into the bulky, cumbersome owl costume hadn't been easy. Getting it out again probably wouldn't be easy, either. Which no doubt explained why Silas was meandering around the yard instead of helping.

Nick wasn't hurrying to lend a hand, either. Tesla noticed he was staring into the cloudless summer sky, a blank look on his face.

"You're trying to think of a way to get the computer back on, aren't you?" Tesla said.

"No," Nick said. But then he sighed. "Not anymore, anyway. I give up."

He trudged over to the dummy and glumly began tugging at one of its boots.

Tesla sifted through the feathers on the superhero costume, found the zipper that ran down the front, and unzipped it. She started pulling one of the dummy's stuffed arms out of the sleeve while DeMarco worked on the other.

"So, DeMarco," Tesla said, "did you notice the time? It's almost—"

"She's coming," DeMarco said.

"Sure, she is," Tesla said. "It's just that she was supposed to come yesterday, and the day before that, and the day before that . . ."

"She's coming."

The boot Nick was pulling on popped off, and he turned his attention to the one still stuck on the dummy's other foot.

"It's not that we don't believe you about your aunt being a movie producer who's working with Cash Ashkinos," Nick said.

"And it's totally believable that they're shooting a scene of the new Metalman movie here in Half Moon Bay," added Tesla.

"And it's great that she offered to take us all to

the movie set to meet the stars," Nick continued. "But—"

"*She's coming*," DeMarco snapped. "I don't know what's been going on with her this week, but the crew is in town, and my aunt is a movie producer, and she *will* take us to the set!"

"Right, fine, of course," Tesla said.

"Absolutely, positively, whatever you say," said Nick.

"She! Is! Coming!" DeMarco retorted.

For a moment, there was only silence, punctuated by the tweeting of backyard birds and the hissing of the neighbors' lawn sprinklers. The three friends tugged at the stunt dummy, with nobody sure what to say next.

Then a woman's voice called out: "DeMarco!"

Everyone turned to look up the long, sloping yard to the house at the top. They could see Mrs. Davison—DeMarco and Elesha and Monique's mother—standing on the back porch.

"DeMarco!" she repeated. "Elesha! Monique! Come up to the house! Your Aunt Zoe is here!"

DeMarco hopped to his feet and began dancing around Nick and Tesla (and Michael-slash-Bald

Eagle).

"I tooooooold ya, but ya didn't belieeeeeeve me," he sang. "I tooooooold ya, but ya didn't belieeeeeeve me."

"Yes, we did," Tesla said.

"Well, I didn't," said Nick.

Silas came tromping out of the woods like a charging rhino. "She's here! She's here!" he shouted. "Quick! Help me pack up all the props!"

"What? Why?" Tesla asked.

"So we can show 'em to Cash Ashkinos, of course! He loves real old-school effects! He's always saying in interviews that they're better than CGI—that's computer-generated imagery. Even if my movie's not done, at least I can show him how I'm going to make it."

Tesla started to object. "He won't have time to look at—" But before she could finish, she had to jump out of the way as Silas skidded to a stop right in front of her.

"Grab the props!" he blurted out. Then he snatched up the half-naked stunt dummy, threw it over his shoulder, and lumbered off toward the house.

"Who's ready for some movie magic?"

Aunt Zoe was looking at DeMarco, her nephew, seated next to her in the front of her Prius. But it was Silas, who was directly behind DeMarco, who quickly answered, "I am! I am!" He bounced in his seat so much that his box of movie props nearly fell off his lap and onto Nick, who was sitting next to him. Which caused Nick to nearly clunk heads with Tesla, who was sitting next to *him*. (The backseat was a tight fit for three people if one of them was Silas.) Luckily, Elesha and Monique were in a different car, driven by their mom; they planned to stop at the Li'l Darlin' Beauty Center because the girls wanted to look their best if they were going to be on a movie set and maybe get discovered by a casting agent. Also luckily, they had all convinced Silas to leave behind Michael the stunt dummy, carefully leaning against a tree in DeMarco's yard.

"So, DeMarco," Aunt Zoe said, "how's your summer been go—?"

"Great, wonderful, he's having the time of his life," Silas said, interrupting her. "You know what I love about Cash Ashkinos movies?"

"Uhh, what?" Aunt Zoe said.

"Cash doesn't fake everything with computers. He *does* it. For real. If two guys are fighting on top of a runaway train about to go off a bridge, then two guys *actually* fight on top of a runaway train about to go off a bridge."

"*Off the Rails 2*," Nick said. He wasn't a movie freak like Silas, or a wannabe stuntman like DeMarco, but he was an eleven-year-old boy, which meant he'd seen his fair share of action flicks.

"If a guy on a burning hang-glider is chased by a helicopter through a tunnel, then a guy on a burning hang-glider is chased by a helicopter through a tunnel," Silas continued.

"*Cut to the Chase 4*," said Nick.

Tesla groaned and rolled her eyes. She was too polite to say so in front of Aunt Zoe, who'd worked on Cash Ashkinos's last five or six movies, but the truth was, she couldn't stand action flicks. Every one of them ignored the laws of physics—and Tesla took the laws of physics very, *very* seriously.

"If a half-man, half-robot superhero flies around with a jet pack and fires rockets out of his hands, then a half-man, half-robot superhero flies around with a jet pack and fires rockets out of his hands," Silas said.

"Hmm," said Nick. "That's in a Cash Ashkinos movie?"

Tesla gave him a look as if to say, "Duh."

"Yeah," she said. "The one he's shooting right now."

"Oh! Of course! *The Stupefying Metalman!*"

"That's how I know this Metalman movie is gonna be the best ever," Silas said, leaning so far forward that he was practically talking right in Aunt Zoe's ear. "The ones they made before, with Richard Johns-Ford III as Metalman, were okay, but they were all wall-to-wall CGI. Every big action scene was just cartoons fighting cartoons. But Cash Ashkinos, he's finally gonna give us a *real* Metalman, am I right?"

Aunt Zoe glanced over at DeMarco with wide eyes. "Is he always like this?" she asked.

DeMarco nodded.

Silas nodded, too.

"Well, Cash is going to try," she said. "You have to understand. The movies Cash and I have been making up to now are what they used to call B-pictures.

You have less money to work with, but more freedom. This is our biggest project yet—it could finally get Cash onto the A list—but a budget this large means that you have to . . . make compromises."

"What kinds of compromises?" Silas asked.

Aunt Zoe brought the car to a stop at a red light. On the other side of a busy road—the famous Pacific Coast Highway that runs up and down the western edge of California—was downtown Half Moon Bay. It was a small, cute, quaint town that catered to tourists and surfers. It had been a pretty quiet and laid-back place, at least until Nick and Tesla showed up.

"I grew up here, you know," Aunt Zoe said. "Every Saturday, I'd ride my bike downtown and watch whatever movie was playing at the Veranda Theater. It was a tiny cinema in a tiny town, and everything up on the screen seemed so much bigger than the world I knew. I wanted to be a part of that. My senior year of high school, they closed the Veranda, but I never forgot what it was like to sit in that little boxy dark theater and *dream*. And now I'm back, and we've opened up the Veranda again and are using it as a location in a movie that *I'm* producing. At the end of the day, we even use the screening room to watch the raw footage we shot. My dreams have come true."

What followed was a long, thoughtful silence.

Just as Nick was about to say "That was really inspiring," Silas spoke up.

"You didn't answer my question," he said.

Tesla leaned forward to see past Nick and glare at her clueless friend.

"What?" Silas said. "She didn't."

The light turned green, and Aunt Zoe hit the gas. The Prius shot across the highway into downtown Half Moon Bay.

"Cash is a visionary," Aunt Zoe said. "But if you're interested in making movies, Silas, you have to learn that filmmaking is a collaborative art. It requires the creative input of dozens of people. There has to be give-and-take. There has to be flexibility. There have to be compromises. That's just how it works."

Another thoughtful silence.

Which Silas once again broke.

"Yeah," he said, "but *what* compromises?"

Nick, Tesla, and DeMarco groaned.

"The ones you have to make to keep the right people happy," Aunt Zoe said, sounding as if she'd finally lost her patience. But then she added, more softly, "Because when the wrong people aren't happy—what the . . . ?"

The car had turned off Main Street and onto Correas Street, not far from the old abandoned Veranda Theater. Halfway up the block, the street was closed off, with traffic cones and sawhorses and, just beyond them, an assortment of trucks and trailers and generators and equipment.

Clearly, this was where Cash Ashkinos and his crew were filming *The Stupefying Metalman*. But just in case there'd been any doubt, a group of a half dozen or so people, some wearing costumes, was standing across the street from the blocked-off area. "Looks like some fans of Metalman are here," Tesla said. But then she noticed the signs they were waving. They read:

"METALMAN, GO HOME!!!"

3

There were NO PARKING signs taped to the meters up and down the block, but Aunt Zoe parked next to one anyway. As everyone got out of the car, she put a slip of pink paper on the dashboard. Most of the area around the movie theater was blocked off by trailers, sawhorses, temporary fences, and traffic cones. A man in a security guard uniform waved to Aunt Zoe, then gestured at the protestors across the street and shrugged miserably.

The protestors waved their signs more vigorously and started chanting something.

"Hey," Silas said, "I know them."

"Why am I not surprised?" Aunt Zoe muttered. She suddenly sounded very, very tired, as if she wanted to crawl underneath the car and go to sleep.

"Who are they?" asked Nick.

Six people stood across the street—four men and two women, ranging in age from late teens to Really Old. ("Really Old" was about as specific as Nick could get if a person was older than his parents.) A few wore shorts and T-shirts; the others looked to be sporting homemade superhero costumes. One of the women appeared to be dressed as some kind of pirate cat.

Silas raised a hand and began pointing at each of the protestors.

"There's Stellan Something, Casey Something—Stellan and Casey are brothers. Rude Batman Fan, Smelly Spider-Man Fan, Anime Girl. Oh, and look, a lady dressed as Captain Bloodwhiskers, from the Japanese cartoon *Hamburger Cloud Rainbow Police*."

"Huh?" Aunt Zoe said.

"Customers," said DeMarco. "From Hero Worship Incorporated."

"The local comic book shop," Tesla explained. "Silas's dad owns it."

"Great. Just great," said Aunt Zoe.

"If they're comic book fans, why do they hate Metalman?" Nick asked Silas.

"They don't, as far as I know," Silas said. "In fact, the Something brothers love him. He's their favorite superhero. They've offered my dad, like, a thousand bucks for the Metalman statue in front of his store."

"So, it's weird that they'd protest a Metalman movie," Tesla said, "*and* it's weird that they'd know one was filming in town. DeMarco told us it was a big secret."

Aunt Zoe sighed.

"It is a big secret. We've been telling people we're here shooting *Santa Claus vs. the Zombies*."

"Oooh! Good title!" Silas said.

"But it's no surprise that word got out," Aunt Zoe continued. She jerked her chin at the protestors. "Or that they're here. There's the Internet, after all. Oh, well. Time to face the music. Come on." She started walking toward the gap between the fences and sawhorses, where the security guard was standing.

"You should probably leave that in the car," Tesla said to Silas, who was struggling with his box of props.

"If I leave it in the car, I can't show it to Cash!"

"Sure you can. You can come back and get it once you've set up a meeting with him. Till then, you don't want to be lugging it all over the place, like some kind of . . ."

Tesla tried to remember what the people were called who ran around movie sets doing all the grunt work. She knew they had a specific title—she'd read it once in a news article—but the word just wouldn't come to her.

So she just said "flunky."

"Welllll . . . I guess you're right," Silas said. He looked down at the animatronic arm sticking out of the box.

"Don't worry. You'll meet Cash," Silas said to the arm. "I promise."

He slid the box onto the backseat.

"Thanks," DeMarco whispered to Tesla.

As Aunt Zoe led everyone toward the set, the protestors began chanting louder than ever.

"We're comics fans, through and through!" the one dressed as Captain Bloodwhiskers called out.

"And Damon Wilder will not do!" the other protestors chanted back.

"Damon Wilder's going to be the new Metalman," DeMarco explained to Tesla. "My sisters are nuts about him because he once guest-starred on *The Witches of Greenwich Village*, on the Disney Channel. But mostly he's done boring movies where people just sit around and talk. Like *The Wisdom of the Trembling Butterfly*. I watched five minutes of that on the Film Channel because I thought it was a martial arts movie. Boy, did it stink. I think the whole story happens in a coffeehouse."

"One-two-three-four-five!" yelled Captain Bloodwhiskers.

"Casting Damon Wilder's jive!"

"Six-seven-eight-nine-ten!"

"Fire him and start again!"

"They may be nuts," DeMarco admitted, "but they do good chants."

"What do they have against Damon Wilder?" said Nick.

Tesla shrugged.

Aunt Zoe threw them a grim look.

"You two don't spend a lot of time on the Internet, do you?"

Before Nick could admit that, in fact, he'd been spending way too much time on the Internet lately but still didn't know what was going on, the protestors finally recognized Silas.

"For shame!" the one he'd called Casey Something shouted at him.

"Traitor!" shouted Casey's brother, Stellan Something.

"You stink, Kuskie!" roared Rude Batman Fan.

"They're just jealous," Silas said, and he gave a jaunty wave as Aunt Zoe walked him and the others past the protestors, around the sawhorses and traffic cones, and onto the set.

Aunt Zoe paused to consult with the security guard and a woman standing next to him.

"When did they show up?" she said, jerking a thumb over her shoulder.

"About ten minutes ago," the guard said.

"There's been another leak," the woman added. She was a twenty-something and wore a baseball cap and a grungy T-shirt printed with the words ASK ME ABOUT MY SCREENPLAY.

"Obviously," Aunt Zoe said with a sigh. "And today was going so well, too . . ."

The protestors launched into another round of "Hey! Yo! Whadaya know?"

"Leak?" Tesla said.

Uh-oh, thought Nick.

During the drive to the movie set, he'd decided that Tesla was right. He was dealing with their parents' disappearance by obsessing about it. But he also knew that Tesla had her own way of distracting herself from the situation: by poking her nose into every problem she could find. Or at least that's how Nick saw it. And he could tell by the tone of her voice that she was shifting into nose-poking mode.

Fortunately (again, as Nick saw it), no one reacted to Tesla's question.

"Let 'em yell all they want," Aunt Zoe said to the guard. "We aren't doing any dialogue scenes this afternoon anyway, so it won't make any difference." She turned to the woman. "Tell them I'm headed to introduce my guests to Cash. Oh, and my sister will be here soon with my nieces, so just give me a call when they arrive."

There was a shrill, high-pitched squeal behind Aunt Zoe.

"Did you actually just say 'squee'?" DeMarco whispered to Silas.

Silas just grinned maniacally and rubbed his hands together.

The turtleneck woman nodded at Aunt Zoe; then she snatched a walkie-talkie clipped to her belt and started talking fast into it.

"Zoe Helms has landed and is flushing guests. She's on her way to Video Village."

"Come on," Aunt Zoe said, and she led the kids away from the protestors.

"Landed?" asked Tesla.

"Flushing guests?" asked Nick.

"Video Village?" asked DeMarco.

"Squee!" said Silas.

Aunt Zoe guided them around one of the big semitrailers lining the blocked-off street.

"That's all just industry slang," she explained. "'Landed' means I've arrived. 'Flushing' means I'm moving someone or something across the set. And 'Video Village' is where the camera department sets up monitors, so the D.P. and the director and producers can watch what's being shot."

"The T.P.?" asked Nick.

Aunt Zoe chuckled.

"Sorry. More slang. The D.P. is the director of photography. He or she is in charge of the camera department and the overall look of the movie."

"And what was that lady back there, with the security guard?" Tesla said.

"Abby? Oh, she's a P.A. Production assistant."

"That's what I was trying to think of! Production assistant!" Tesla said. "The flunkies!"

Aunt Zoe threw her a look that was half amused, half horrified.

"I wouldn't say that too loudly if I were you," she said, keeping her own voice low. "There are P.A.s everywhere."

The group stepped around the end of the trailer, and Tesla could see how true that was.

Ringed around them were big trailers, small trailers, food tables, picnic tables, burly guys lugging equipment, zombies eating doughnuts (*zombies eating doughnuts?*), and, weaving through it all, a small army of male and female P.A.s, most clad in shorts and colorful shirts and either talking into walkie-talkies or listening intently to someone who was.

Naturally, Silas *squeed* again.

"Please, stop doing that," DeMarco told him.

"Welcome to Hollywood, kids," Aunt Zoe said. "Or, at least, as close to Hollywood as Half Moon Bay is ever going to get. This way."

The group got some curious stares as they passed the trailers and tables and burly guys and zombies, but not many. Everyone was way too busy to take much interest in the field trip Aunt Zoe seemed to be leading.

"I'll eventually need to get you set passes from the production office," Aunt Zoe said. "But for now it's okay, so long as you stick close to me."

They walked briskly through the hustle and bustle and around another trailer. "And here we are! Our main location today: the Veranda!"

Aunt Zoe spread her arms wide. Before them was what had been Half Moon Bay's dilapidated, long-abandoned movie theater. No longer was the box office boarded up or the doors chained shut or the lobby dusty and bare. Now, everything sparkled, everything shined. When yet another P.A. burst through the doors and hurried outside talking brusquely into her walkie-talkie, the smell of fresh-popped popcorn wafted outside.

The usual message on the marquee—CLOS D, set in faded, crooked letters—had been replaced with STREETRACE 5: THE SPEED YOU NEED.

"Ha!" said Silas, pointing up at the sign. "That's an old Cash Ashkinos movie! Get it?"

"Never mind that, dude!" said DeMarco. "That's Cash Ashkinos!"

He pointed out a tall, lanky man wearing cowboy boots, aviator sunglasses, black jeans, and a tight, blindingly white T-shirt. His long, craggy face was covered with carefully trimmed hair that was too short to be a beard yet too thick to be considered whiskers or stubble. It looked like strips of brown moss that had been pasted to his cheeks and chin.

"Whoa, you're right," Silas said. "It's him." Silas's voice faded to a whisper, as if he was afraid of breaking a magical spell. "It's really him."

Ashkinos was about twenty yards away, talking to another man in what Tesla guessed was "Video Village." The two of them were surrounded by tall, canvas-backed director chairs, and as they spoke they peered into a bank of video monitors stacked in front of them.

"So, now we can have our meeting?" Silas said. "I mean—now we meet Cash?"

Aunt Zoe shook her head.

"Not yet. It looks like he's planning the next camera setup with our visual effects supervisor. They should be about to shoot a scene where a theater full of zombified townspeople rush out and attack Metalman."

"Damon Wilder will be here?"

"No, he's done for the day. The Metalman in this scene can be computer generated. We'll add it in postproduction."

"'We'll add it in postproduction'?" repeated a disbelieving Silas. "That's not how Cash Ashkinos shoots an action movie. He works with real people, real props, *real* danger."

"This is a different kind of action movie, Silas," Aunt Zoe said with a shrug. "A really expensive one," she added under her breath.

"That boy's right, Zoe," said a deep, booming voice behind them. "Why use a computer-generated hero when you've got the real thing right here?"

Everyone turned to see a towering, armor-clad man clanking directly toward them. He was encased in blue and silver metal from his toes to his jutting chin, but his head was bare, revealing a squared jaw, rugged cheekbones, and perfectly styled blond hair. He carried a gleaming helmet under one arm and smiled confidently as he strode toward Zoe and the kids.

"Metalman!" Silas said, clapping his hands in delight.

And it *was* Metalman. Or a man in a Metalman costume, anyway.

But Aunt Zoe was less than delighted.

"Kill me now," she said, groaning in dismay.

Only Nick and Tesla seemed to hear Aunt Zoe's groan or notice the look of horror on her face. Everyone else in their tour group was too excited by the sudden arrival of an honest-to-goodness star.

Silas and DeMarco didn't *squee*, but they did stare in wide-eyed surprise. The armor-covered man tromping toward them was *The Stupefying Metalman*'s lead actor, Damon Wilder.

Tesla nudged her brother and nodded at some of the crew members milling about. They looked as surprised to see him as everyone else did. But they also looked a lot less pleased.

"Step aside, citizens," Wilder said, parting the kids with a sweep of his free arm. "I have work to do."

And with that, he marched past, nodding to Zoe, and headed for Video Village.

When Cash Ashkinos noticed the actor coming in his direction, he clenched his jaw and pressed a hand to his forehead, as if he'd just been hit by an instantaneous migraine.

"Cry havoc," Wilder intoned gravely as he

stomped up to Ashkinos. "And let slip the circuits of war!"

"That doesn't sound like Metalman," Silas said.

"It's Shakespeare," Nick said. "Except for the 'circuits' part."

"That's the problem," Aunt Zoe sighed.

"What do you mean?" Tesla asked.

Aunt Zoe sucked in a long, deep breath.

"Sorry. Duty calls," she said. "You guys wait here. I'll be back."

With obvious reluctance, Zoe headed for Video Village, where Ashkinos was talking to Wilder in a low tone.

"But I'm here!" Wilder broke in, making no effort to keep his voice low. "I can confront the zomboids!"

Ashkinos started murmuring again to Wilder, and when Aunt Zoe reached them, she joined in.

"A computer-generated Metalman? We'll add it in post?" Wilder was yelling at them. "I can't believe I'm hearing this! I thought you were the director who did everything for real!"

"Yeah," Silas said to DeMarco. "That's what I thought."

DeMarco shrugged. "You know I'm big into

stunts, but it's probably hard to do a flying half-robot superhero for real."

Tesla noticed that a little cluster of P.A.s had gathered around, lingering to eavesdrop on the argument.

"What's that all about?" she asked the nearest P.A., a man with a shaved head and dark sunglasses. He opened his mouth to answer.

But then he shut it.

"No comment," said one of the other P.A.s.

"What's what all about?" said another.

Suddenly P.A.s were flying off in all directions.

Several threw quick, fearful looks over their shoulders in the direction of another man who'd just walked up. He had curly brown hair and a round, tanned face, a twisted smirk settling on his lips. In one hand he carried a paper bag, into which he kept dipping to shove some kind of crunchy chips in his mouth.

"What's it all about?" he said to Tesla. "Great acting, that's what."

He spoke loudly, as if Tesla were a ninety-year-old woman with bad hearing. Tesla wondered why, until she realized that his words were meant to be overheard.

"Jack Wiltrout, everybody!" Wilder called to the newcomer. "Jack! Come here and back me up!"

Jack gave the kids a wink and a smarmy smile. "You might want to get my autograph later," he said. "It's gonna be worth something one day."

He paused to chew on some chips. Then he walked off toward Wilder.

As the man drew closer, Wilder turned back to Ashkinos and Aunt Zoe, who were standing shoulder to shoulder facing him, frowning.

"Jack's written some dynamite new dialogue for this scene," Wilder said. "Listen to this. The zomboids come running out of the movie theater screaming and wailing, and when I see them I say: 'How ironic. I, a man of unfeeling metal, must save these souls who are caught between life and death. And yet I remain neither wholly man nor wholly machine, neither live nor dead. My soul forever trapped in an existential limbo.'"

Wilder pressed his palm against his forehead as he finished the last line, holding that position for a few seconds. Then he dropped his arm and turned to Ashkinos, saying, "Annnd scene!"

"*What* kind of limbo?" asked Silas. "Does he mean the Lifeless Limbo of Dimension L, where Metalman fought the Unliving Limbo Legion?"

"I don't think so," said DeMarco.

Meanwhile, Jack Wiltrout joined the conversation over in Video Village.

"Metalman's internal conflict about his raison d'être is central to the character," he was saying. "The fanboys'll eat it up." He noticed some crumbs on his shirt and quickly brushed them to the ground.

Aunt Zoe and Ashkinos threw each other looks that made it plain they didn't think *anyone* would find that idea appetizing.

"If we shoot this scene with you, Damon," Ashkinos said, his voice low and soothing, "I think we should just stick to the script."

With a clang, Wilder slapped his metal-covered hands together.

"Perfect! Let's roll, then!" he said, clearly choosing to ignore the "if" that had begun Ashkinos's last sentence. "Makeup! Props!"

Crew members began to approach, reluctantly, carrying various cosmetics paraphernalia.

"Why do you need makeup?" Ashkinos asked.

"You're going to be wearing your helmet in this scene."

"I think I should take it off before I speak," Wilder replied. "I mean, you do want the audience to know it's me, right? Otherwise, you could just use a special effect."

Ashkinos simply glowered at the actor. A moment later, he glanced toward the crew and gave them a curt nod. A man stepped up and took the helmet from Wilder while a woman swooped in and began patting his face with what looked like a small sponge.

"Just a little mattifying powder across the cheeks, Barbara," the actor said. "My skin doesn't need much help in natural light."

The woman muttered, threw the sponge back into the black cosmetics case she was carrying, and pulled out a small round brush.

"Why don't we do it once your way and once my way, hmm?" Cash Ashkinos said as the makeup artist began dusting Wilder with "mattifying powder," whatever that was. "Once where the helmet comes off, once where it stays on. Then, later, we see which one plays better."

Wilder gave him a suspicious look, but smiled.

"Sure. Give and take, that's what it's all about," he said. "Speaking of which, Jack's got some other ideas we could try out. We need more *frisson*, more panache. The dialogue in the script sounds like it was written by a twelve-year-old."

"Hey!" Silas said. "What's he talking about? I'm twelve and I write great dialogue. Remember the scene where Bald Eagle is wounded by Lady Evil-ika, and he says, 'Don't worry, she only winged me?' That was good enough to have been written by a thirteen-year-old!"

"Does Damon Wilder seem like kind of a nut to you?" DeMarco whispered.

"I don't know about nut, but jerk, definitely," said Silas.

Tesla leaned in close to her brother.

"I think I'm beginning to see why Zoe kept putting off the set visit," she whispered.

"Because it's such a long walk from the parking area?" Nick whispered back.

Tesla glared at him.

"I don't mean that. I'm talking about—"

She jerked her head in Damon Wilder's direction. "*Him.*"

"Oh," said Nick.

Nick eyed the actor, who was telling Ashkinos, "You've got to let me monologue, Cash. We'll never get deep into Metalman's persona if I can't monologue," as Barbara the makeup artist dusted his face.

Aunt Zoe was looking profoundly unhappy.

"Wilder does seem kind of, um, intense," said Nick. "But I don't know. Isn't that what actors are *supposed* to be like?"

"It's more than just the way he's acting," Tesla said. "There were those protestors, too. How did they find out that this is a Metalman movie? And what do they have against Wilder?"

Nick gave his sister a long-suffering look.

"A guy's walking around downtown Half Moon Bay in a Metalman outfit, Tez. Even with guards to keep people off the set, someone's gonna notice sooner or later. And Metalman fans need only one reason to dislike Wilder: He's not Richard Johns-Ford III."

Tesla shook her head.

"I think there's more to it than that. Something weird is going on around here."

Silas and DeMarco sidled up beside their friends.

"Did I just hear you say, 'Something weird is going on around here'?" DeMarco asked, keeping his voice low.

He threw a nervous glance at his aunt, who had placed herself between Wilder and Ashkinos and seemed to be trying to calm them both down.

"'Cuz I know what happens after you say that," DeMarco said. "The weird just keeps getting weirder and weirder until the cops show up."

"I swear, girlfriend," Silas said to Tesla. "You could find a mystery just going to the fridge for a Coke."

Tesla, Nick, and DeMarco gaped at him.

"*Girlfriend?*" Tesla said.

Silas blinked.

"I'm just trying to have a little more sass. Like Blake 'The Brick' Anderson, the wisecracking cop in *The Quick and the Curious 3*. You don't like it?"

"No," Tesla said.

"Anyway," said DeMarco, "please don't try to turn this into some kind of adventure. You know I'm usually up for that, but not when my aunt might find out and tell my mom."

Tesla folded her arms across her chest.

"I'm not trying to turn anything into an adventure. I'm just noticing that something's weird."

Silas swiped a hand at her.

"It's show biz, baby. It wouldn't be normal if it wasn't weird."

When Silas saw the look on Tesla's face, he added hastily, "No 'baby,' either. Got it."

As the kids talked, the makeup artist finished touching up Wilder's look. Ashkinos led the actor off to a spot in front of the theater, speaking to him in a low but intense tone.

"Yes. I see. Got it. Perfect," Wilder said, nodding.

A prop guy trailed behind, fiddling with the silver helmet as he walked.

Meanwhile, several crew members had taken up position in front of the movie theater. One had a bulky camera perched on his shoulder. Another was holding a long pole with what looked like a fluffy throw pillow stuck onto the end of it. (This was in fact a microphone, covered to keep the wind from causing unwanted noise.)

"Ready inside?" yet another crew member said into his walkie-talkie.

A burst of static followed, and then a woman's voice barked back, "Ready!"

The man with the walkie-talkie gave Ashkinos a thumbs-up.

Ashkinos patted Wilder on the back and then turned and stalked off. As he left, the man holding the helmet stepped up, helped Wilder put it on, and then jogged away as well.

"Roll sound," Ashkinos said to a woman sitting near Video Village and fiddling with electronic equipment.

"Sound speed," she said.

"Roll camera," said Ashkinos.

"Camera speed," said the guy holding the camera.

One of the crew members who was huddled beside the cameraman then leaned in front of the camera, holding out a black-and-white board with glowing red numbers.

"Marker. Scene thirty, take one," she said. She lifted a ruler-like length of wood attached to the top of the board with a single bolt and then slapped it down with a *clack!*

"Action!" said Ashkinos.

"Cool," Silas and DeMarco whispered in unison, mesmerized.

Tesla was about to shush them, but whatever

she might have said would have been drowned out by the howls of the drooling, green-skinned "zomboids" now staggering out of the movie theater. Once a good twenty or thirty of the undead had reached the sidewalk, the cameraman swiveled to point his lens toward a lone shiny figure, arms akimbo and legs spread wide, standing farther up the block.

Tesla wasn't really into comic books or action movies, but even she had to admit the whole experience was pretty amazing. They were about to see Metalman (or at least a guy dressed like Metalman) confront a rampaging zombified horde. It was easy to believe that she was watching a crowd infected with an alien zombie virus, instead of a bunch of actors in green goopy makeup.

"Remember what Zoe said in the car?" Nick whispered to her. "It really is like a dream." Tesla agreed. Whatever weirdness might be going on around that movie set, this moment was magical.

"The fault, Lord Computron," Wilder was saying, his voice tinged with a trace of British accent, "lies in our—hey!"

And then Metalman began to twitch and shiver.

"Hey," Wilder repeated. This time the shiver was

a full-on convulsion. "Hey!"

"I can see why he wanted to change the dialogue," Silas whispered. "That's terrible."

Wilder was jerking in a circle, his hands desperately clawing at his armor.

"Ooo! Ow! Hey!" he yelped.

Then the actor dropped to the pavement, shuddering and jerking wildly.

"That isn't dialogue!" Tesla shouted, bursting into a dash toward the fallen Wilder. "Something's gone horribly wrong!"

Nick, Silas, and DeMarco looked at one another.

They were standing on a movie set watching a scene being filmed, and they really, really didn't want to get thrown off because they had freaked out and ran in front of the camera.

On the other hand, they couldn't imagine a Metalman movie in which the hero is supposed to confront a bunch of zombies and say "Ooo! Ow! Hey!" and then have a seizure. And even if that was how the scene was supposed to go, Tesla had already ruined it by running to Damon Wilder's side.

On the *other* other hand, none of the dozens of adults standing around were moving in to check on the quivering actor. Which suggested that this shaking fit was in the script.

On the *other* other other hand—

"Well, come on!" Tesla called back over her shoulder.

And with that, all the boys sprinted after her.

"DeMarco! What are you doing?" Aunt Zoe called out.

"I have no idea!" DeMarco said.

When the boys caught up to Tesla, she was kneeling beside the writhing, thrashing costume-covered man, her hands holding onto his gleaming metal helmet.

"So, what *are* we doing?" Silas asked.

"I think there's something wrong with his armor!" Tesla said, tugging on the helmet.

"Get it off me! Get it off me!" Wilder screamed.

"Help me take it off him!" Tesla said.

"My skin! My skin!" Wilder was screeching now.

Nick took hold of the helmet and started tugging along with Tesla, while Silas grabbed one of Wilder's

boots and DeMarco grabbed the other.

"Man, this stuff is on tight," Silas groused as he yanked fruitlessly on the boot. "It's like he's welded into it."

"Ow! Hey! Don't pull my foot off!" Wilder howled.

"Sorry," Silas said.

Wilder went back to shrieking about his skin.

"Why aren't the grown-ups helping?" DeMarco asked.

Indeed, the crew members and zomboids and everyone else were still standing around staring. Then Aunt Zoe and Cash Ashkinos started walking toward them—slowly, cautiously.

"Is this improv?" Ashkinos asked. "I'm starting to think there's really something wrong with him."

"I don't know." Aunt Zoe said. She sounded concerned. "It could be more method."

"No, this isn't acting!" Wilder wailed. "Even I'm not this good! Ahhhhhhh!"

Then the prop man dashed up next to Silas and helped him yank one of Metalman's shiny boots. It tore loose with the sound of crumpling metal and ripping fabric.

"Watch it with the suit," the prop guy said. "That

thing cost $100,000."

"It's like I'm on fire!" Wilder cried. "On fire!"

Cash Ashkinos sighed. He didn't look scared or worried. Just annoyed.

"A hundred grand is cheap compared to Wilder," he said. "Get the suit off him as fast as you can, Matt."

"You're the boss."

Matt—a.k.a. the prop guy—waved back Silas and the other kids. Then he moved to Wilder's head and grasped the helmet. He pulled and twisted. It looked like he was taking Wilder's head off—and it sounded like that, too, from the way the actor yelped. But a moment later, the helmet came free, and Wilder's head remained attached to his neck.

Wilder stared up at the man, wild eyed, red faced, and sweaty.

"It's not my head that's the problem! It's my shoulders! And my back! And my butt! Ahhhhhhh!"

Matt looked up at Ashkinos.

"Do it," Ashkinos said.

Matt began tearing apart the Metalman armor.

"I think somebody put something in the costume," Tesla said to Aunt Zoe. "You should probably get him into a shower when he's finally freed."

Aunt Zoe gave her a quizzical look. She started to reply, but a loud "Oh, my!" cut her off. There were several other gasps, a few chortles, and even a low whistle, all coming from the various crew members, P.A.s, security guards, and various personnel who'd gathered around the scene. Matt was almost done ripping the Metalman suit off the actor. And Wilder, it turned out, was wearing nothing under his costume but a pair of skimpy cotton underwear known far and wide as "tighty-whities." Suddenly a pair of P.A.s came swooping in to help Wilder stand, wrapping him in a robe. Which wasn't easy since Wilder kept scratching wildly at himself.

Nick turned to say something to Tesla but found his sister trying to see over the crowd, craning to get a peek at Wilder.

"What?" she said when she noticed her brother was looking at her. "I wanted to see if he had burns or a rash."

"Did he?"

Tesla shook her head. "Just some scrapes."

It was too late for Nick to steal a peek of his own.

"What happened?" Ashkinos asked his star.

"I don't know!" Wilder said, still scratching. "One second I was hitting my mark, ready to say my lines, and the next my skin was on fire. It's not as bad now that I'm out of that tin can."

"Well, I think you'd probably better go to your trailer," Aunt Zoe said. She threw a quick glance at Tesla. "And a shower seems like a good idea."

"And some rest," Ashkinos added.

He slapped Wilder on the back.

Wilder winced.

"Take whatever time you need, Damon," he said.

"Fine," Wilder said miserably as he left. "But I'll be back, Cash. I can do this scene!"

"Sure. Sure, you can, Damon," Ashkinos said.

As soon as the actor had limped out of earshot, Ashkinos clapped his hands together and rubbed them gleefully.

"All-righty, then—we're back to CGI Metalman."

"Cash," Matt said, holding up the tatters of the Metalman suit, "it's totaled. There's only one good one left now."

"We'll blow up that bridge when we come to it. All right, people! Let's get ready to run it again!"

On the director's order, crew members began

hustling to and fro, and the zombies turned and shuffled back into the movie theater.

"Excuse me," Tesla said to Matt the prop guy, who had started walking away with the ruined costume. "May I take a look at that?"

Matt peered at her from behind his squat square-framed eyeglasses.

"Just who are you, anyway?"

"A guest of Zoe Helms," DeMarco said. "Isn't that right, Aunt Zoe?"

Aunt Zoe hesitated only a moment before saying "yes."

At that moment, Cash Ashkinos walked up and stood next to Aunt Zoe. "I never got a chance to officially meet your guests. That was some impressive reaction time, you guys. Damon was lucky you were so quick to jump in and help him. Otherwise, he might still be lying there itching like crazy." For a second it seemed like Ashkinos was imagining that very scenario, smiling at the idea. But then he quickly held out his arm to shake hands with each of the kids. Silas was last.

"You may as well let her take a look at the armor, Matt," Aunt Zoe said. "It's not like she could ruin the suit any more than it already is."

"That's . . . some grip . . ." Ashkinos was saying to Silas, who was still pumping the director's hand furiously, an idiotic grin plastered on his face. He seemed unwilling to let go.

Matt sighed and then motioned for Tesla to approach, adding in a resigned tone: "Fine. Have at it, kid."

Tesla walked over and began examining the blue and silver armor, especially the black nylon holding it all together.

Nick joined her. Then DeMarco.

Meanwhile, Cash Ashkinos was still trying to pull away from Silas's grip. "If you'll excuse me . . . ," Cash said, "I have to . . . direct . . ." And with a final yank, he pulled his hand free.

For a moment or two, Silas continued to shake an invisible hand in the empty air. "I eagle camera good!" he stammered. "Silas!"

"Okay, then," Cash said. "I'm going over there now. Nice to meet you, Simon."

Meanwhile, Aunt Zoe had joined Tesla and the others, gathered around the pile of Metalman armor.

"See anything?" Aunt Zoe asked.

"Not yet, but—a-ha!"

"A-ha?" repeated Aunt Zoe.

"That usually means she found something," DeMarco explained.

"Umm, yes. I guessed as much," Aunt Zoe said. "But what?"

Tesla pointed at the costume.

"That."

Everyone—even Matt the prop guy—leaned in for a closer look.

There was a group *thonk*, and then everyone leaned out again, rubbing their foreheads.

"Let's try that one at a time," Aunt Zoe said.

One by one, Aunt Zoe, then Matt, then the boys peered into the costume. And one by one they saw a long streak of granular, orange-brown particles ground into the nylon.

"That's on the inside of the costume, right?" Tesla asked Matt.

He nodded.

"Sure. Up around here."

He touched the back of his neck and shoulders.

Tesla and Nick looked at each other.

"Looks like you're not the only one who knows

about [WORD CENSORED BY THE PUBLISHER'S LE-GAL DEPARTMENT]," said Nick.

"[WORD CENSORED BY THE PUBLISHER'S LEGAL DEPARTMENT]?" said Aunt Zoe. "What's that?"

"The main ingredient in itching powder," Nick explained.

Matt scoffed. "Itching powder? That's just some dumb gag in old comic books."

Nick and Tesla shook their heads grimly.

"It isn't?" DeMarco said.

"No. It's real," said Nick. "It's nasty stuff, too. You'd have to be pretty mean to make up a batch and use it on somebody."

He gave his sister a significant look.

"It was just once, okay?!" she blurted out. "And that kid was the worst lab partner in the history of the universe!"

Tesla's admission was followed by a moment of awkward silence.

"Annnyway," Aunt Zoe said, "does the itching powder work immediately?"

"It's instantaneous," Nick said.

Tesla rubbed her chin and narrowed her eyes. "Which means—"

But she was unable to finish her thought.

"Where's my star? My boy? My dear, dear friend?" a voice suddenly wailed behind her. "Is he all right? Sweet Lord in heaven, tell me he's all right!"

Everyone turned to find a white-haired man in a suit running toward them. He wore a panic-stricken expression on a face so tanned and taut that it looked like football leather.

"Damon's fine, Bob," Aunt Zoe said to him. "And he's not here."

"Oh."

The man stopped running, and the fear immediately left his face.

"Where have you been, anyway?" Aunt Zoe asked him. "I need to talk to you."

"You need to talk to me, the studio needs to talk to me, my ex-wives need to talk to me, my ulcers need to talk to me. Everybody needs to talk to me! But will anybody *listen* to me?"

"Bob—"

"You want to know where I was? On the phone. Because the insurance company needed to talk to me, too, thanks to our friend Mr. Internet. 'Don't believe a word of it, Colin,' I'm saying. 'Everything's going great, Colin!' And then some P.A. is running up to tell me that now my leading man is having a heart attack!"

"He didn't have a heart attack. It was just another"—Aunt Zoe's gaze flicked, for just a second, to the kids—"incident."

"Another incident? *Another incident?* I've never seen so many 'incidents' on a set in my life—and I've produced two movies starring a chimpanzee! Is this how you and Ashkinos always operate? Because, let me tell you something, toots—you're in the big leagues now, and it only takes one swing-and-a-miss to strike out!"

"Now, Bob . . . it's not Cash's fault," Aunt Zoe said. She walked over to the man and began speaking to him reassuringly.

"Who's that old guy?" DeMarco asked Matt. He was displeased to see someone talking so harshly to his aunt. "Is that Damon Wilder's dad?"

"No," Matt answered, chuckling a bit. "That's Bob Ortmann. The executive producer."

"I thought Aunt Zoe was the producer," Nick said.

"She's *a* producer. This movie has seven. Or maybe it's eight now. I keep losing track. Anyway, Zoe's the line producer—she manages what's happening on set day to day." Matt nodded at Bob. "He's the executive producer. The money man. If he's not happy, the studio's not happy. And if the studio's not happy, we're all out of a job."

"Itching powder?" Bob said, nearly exploding at Aunt Zoe. His eyes were wide and his hands waved over his head. "*Itching powder?* What is this, a Bugs Bunny cartoon?"

"He doesn't look happy," Silas said.

Matt gathered up the ruined Metalman suit. "If you'll excuse me, I need to see what I can salvage of this," he said. Then he added, under his breath, "And I need to get my resume ready."

"Don't get any of that powder on you," Tesla said.

Matt glanced at her skeptically but walked off,

his pinched fingers carefully holding the tattered costume away from his body.

Meanwhile, Bob was still ranting at Aunt Zoe. She answered in a soft, soothing tone, and he calmed down just a little (this was evident because his face changed from being as red as a fire engine to pink, like a flamingo). "Fine!" he said at last. "Let's call the studio right now, and you can make that promise to 'em yourself!"

Aunt Zoe seemed to mull that idea for a moment, and then she nodded slowly.

"DeMarco, you and your friends wait for me, okay?" she called. "I won't be long."

"Okay," DeMarco said.

Aunt Zoe and Bob walked away together, weaving their way around crew members and equipment.

"You know," Tesla mused, "she didn't tell us *where* to wait."

"I think *here* is what's implied," Nick pointed out.

He knew what was coming, though. And he wasn't the only one.

"I think we should wait wherever *he's* going," DeMarco said, nodding at Matt, who was about thirty yards away. The prop guy was weaving cautiously between the long trailers lining the street, keeping a tight grip on the costume parts but also trying to avoid touching them more than was necessary. At any moment, he might step between two trailers and disappear from sight.

"Come on," Nick said.

"Really?" DeMarco asked.

"Really?" Tesla repeated.

"You were about to say it, anyway," Nick said to his sister. "Right?"

"Right," she said. "Let's go."

"Did I tell you guys I shook hands with Cash Ash-kinos?" Silas said.

The kids were walking single file through the maze of trailers and tents that surrounded Video Village. Nick was in the lead, keeping an eye on Matt, letting the others know when it was safe to move forward. Silas was in the rear.

"We *all* shook hands with Cash Ashkinos," De-Marco said.

"Yeah, but I shook it longer than anyone. And

I told him about my movie and how great it is. He seemed really impressed!" Silas took another half a dozen steps in silence, replaying his golden moment with Cash Ashkinos in his head. Suddenly he blurted out: "Hey! Where are we going?"

"To find out who's messing with my aunt's movie," DeMarco said.

"By following that guy?"

"Itching powder works almost immediately, so it couldn't have been in Damon Wilder's costume when he first showed up," Tesla explained. "It must have been slipped in right before they tried to get that shot."

"But Mr. Wilder was there in front of us the whole time," Silas said.

"Which is how we know that three people touched him right before the camera rolled," Nick said. He started counting on his fingers. "One: the lady who was putting on his makeup. Two: Cash Ashkinos, who patted Wilder on the back. And three—"

"Matt!" Silas burst out, proud to have finally figured out what his friends had known several minutes before.

Up ahead, Matt stopped and looked back.

"Yeah?" he called to the kids.

"Oh, great," Nick muttered.

"Way to go," said DeMarco.

Tesla just voiced a weary sigh and said, "Silas."

But Silas didn't hear them. He'd started walking toward Matt, wearing a big grin on his face.

"We were just wondering—are you the prop master or the costume supervisor?" he said.

"Neither," Matt said. "I'm the special effects supervisor."

Silas's grin widened.

"Really? I love special effects supervisors!"

"Oh, yeah?" Matt said skeptically. "You sure you're not confusing us with *visual* effects supervisors?"

The kids had caught up with him now, and Silas looked like he wanted to drop to the ground and bow at the man's feet.

"No way!" Silas said. "I know the difference. The visual effects guys do all the postproduction stuff. The fake stuff. You do the effects on-set. The cool stuff. Animatronics, stunts, prosthetics, *explosions*. I know most people are more into visual effects these days, but I'm like, 'Forget all that CGI. That's just, like, pushing buttons on a computer. The special effects dudes keep it real!'"

Silas had spoken the magic words. Matt's doubtful frown soon morphed into a smile of delight.

"Wow, kid, you really know your cinema." He held out his hand. "Matt Gore, pleased to meet you. Would you all like to see my shop?"

"Would we?" Silas answered. "I can't think of anything we'd like to do more! Right, guys?"

Silas looked at his friends, who all smiled and nodded enthusiastically.

"Oh, boy!" Nick said.

Tesla elbowed him as a reminder not to lay it on too thick.

"Come on," said Matt. "It's over here."

As he turned and headed between two trailers, Tesla reached out and put a hand on Silas's shoulder.

"I take it all back," she said.

"Take all what back?" Silas asked.

"What I was thinking about you a minute ago."

The kids followed Matt around one corner, then another, and finally up a ramp leading into the back of yet another long white trailer.

"Oh, boy," Nick said again.

Tesla didn't elbow him this time, because she knew he wasn't acting.

Instead she said, "Ditto."

Matt Gore's trailer was like their uncle's basement laboratory, only with fewer test tubes and beakers and a lot more giant robot heads. (Only one giant robot head, actually. But Uncle Newt didn't have any at all, so . . .) There were prop laser rifles and jet packs, animatronic body parts, and work tables covered with paint cans and putty and all sorts of cool-looking tools.

"Hey," Silas said, pointing at the giant head, "is that Lord Computron from the Metalman comics?"

Matt dropped the battered Metalman costume onto the nearest table and put a finger to his lips.

"Shhh. Spoiler alert. We're blowing that up on Thursday."

Silas and DeMarco showed their approval by high-fiving each other.

"Cool, huh?" Nick said to Tesla.

But his eyebrows were saying something very different.

They were waggling up and to the left, signaling, *Look. Over there.*

"Totally!" Tesla enthused, as she tried to steal a peek at whatever her brother was waggling at.

He seemed to be indicating a shelf up so high on the trailer wall that even hulking Silas—who was nearly as tall as Matt—would need to jump just to touch it. The shelf was loaded with plastic bottles and canisters identified with labels like SMOKE–BLACK, SMOKE–WHITE, SMOKE–GRAY and KA-BLAM!

Interesting, but hardly worth a waggle.

But just then, Tesla saw it. At the far end of the shelf stood a small, unlabeled clear-plastic container half filled with orange-brown powder.

Tesla cocked an eyebrow at her brother. *Bingo!*

Then she furrowed her brow slightly, as if trying to signal, *But how do we get it down so we can see if it's itching powder?*

Nick frowned and shrugged. *Got me.*

"I would love to have something like that for *Bald Eagle: The Legend Takes Flight,*" Silas was saying to Matt, still admiring the robotic head. "That's a movie I'm making. I even brought some of the props to show Cash."

Nick and Tesla looked at each other again, and this time their expressions were saying the same thing.

Of course! The arm!

AMAZINGLY ASTONISHING ANIMATRONIC REACHY-GRABBY ROBO-ARM

THE STUFF

- About a dozen regular-size pop sticks (you can get these at a craft store, or just eat a lot of ice pops)

- 5 cable ties

- Epoxy putty (e.g., J-B Weld brand)

- A paint-stirring stick (free at big-box stores)

- Dental floss

- 12 small zip ties

- 6 medium zip ties

- Scissors, wire cutters, or needle-nose pliers

- Hot-glue gun

- Electric drill with a $1/16$-inch bit

- A responsible adult (to help with drilling and mixing the epoxy)

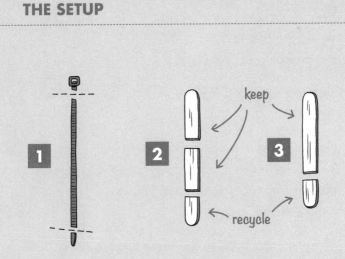

1. Cut the ends off the cable ties so that you're left with 5 pieces that are 4 inches (10 cm) long. Set these aside.

2. Cut 5 of the pop sticks in two, and then trim each piece to 1½ inches (4 cm) long, preserving one rounded end. (You can cut the sticks with scissors, but it's easier to use wire cutters or the cutting part of needle-nose pliers.) You can recycle the trimmings.

3. Trim 5 more pop sticks to 2½ inches (6 cm); recycle the trimmings.

4. Ask an adult to drill a hole into the rounded end of each of the 1½-inch sticks.

5. Use the hot glue to secure 2 short and 1 long pop-stick pieces to a cable tie, as shown. Be sure to leave a ¼-inch (0.75 cm) gap between the sticks.

longest piece

6. Repeat steps 4 and 5 to create 5 "fingers."

7. Have an adult mix the epoxy putty, following the instructions carefully. Form the putty into a blob. (Note: Some epoxies require you to wear gloves.)

8. Stick the fingers you've just made into the epoxy blob "hand"; push the ends that are not drilled approximately ¾ inch (2 cm) into the putty. Note that the thumb should stick out of the palm, as shown in Final Steps, so that it wil lbend toward the other fingers. Insert the paint-stirring stick into the other end of the hand; this will be the arm.

9. The putty can take 10 minutes or more to begin hardening. Before it is fully set, arrange the fingers and thumb exactly where you want them. Be sure to place the thumb opposite the other fingers so that the hand can grip.

10. Cut a 20-inch (50 cm) piece of dental floss and tie it through the hole at the top of one finger. Dental floss is slippery, so make 4 or 5 knots to ensure that it stays in place.

11. Repeat step 10 for each finger and the thumb.

12. Place the small zip ties around the gaps between the sticks that make up the fingers. Make sure they wrap *around* the floss and the larger cable ties. Secure the zip ties, but DO NOT OVERTIGHTEN! Each zip tie should be just tight enough to stay in place but loose enough that the floss moves freely as the fingers bend.

13. Repeat step 12 for each finger and the thumb.

14. Use scissors or wire cutters to trim the ends of the zip ties.

THE FINAL STEPS

---

1. Place a zip tie around the base of the thumb and a cable tie around the base of the wrist. Before you tighten the ties, make sure that they are wrapped around all the floss, as shown.

2. Pull all the floss together and wrap the loose ends around a few pop sticks; then tie a knot to secure them in place. This will be the handle that will control the grip of the animatronic arm.

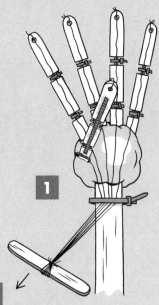

3. Your robo-arm is now ready! Pull down the handle—away from the hand—and the fingers will close and grip. Release, and the hand will open.

4. Start reaching and grabbing! Experiment with light objects first to learn how much weight the hand can handle. Try building others with arms and fingers of different lengths.

"Would *you* like to see some of our props, Mr. Gore?" Tesla said.

"Well, I'm sure they're cool and everything," Matt said. "I used to make my own props and movies when I was your age. But I am at work here, so . . ."

Tesla put on a pout.

Nick helped out with sad puppy eyes.

"Oh, okay, why not." Matt said. "Cash is using a CG Metalman in the next shot anyway, so I'm not as busy as I should be—I mean, *could* be."

"Great! I'll be right back!" Tesla

said. "Come on, DeMarco. I need you to get the keys to your aunt's car."

"Sure."

DeMarco followed Tesla down the ramp leading out of the trailer. When they had left Matt far enough behind, he turned to Tesla and said, "Why do you *really* need me? Aunt Zoe didn't lock her car."

"Here's the plan," Tesla said. She didn't have a plan yet. But by the time she was done talking, she did.

Knowing that it would take a few minutes for Tesla and DeMarco to return with the robo-arm, Nick decided to put the time to good use.

He may not have been as enthusiastic about solving mysteries as his sister was; the puzzle he really wanted to figure out was of the one involving their parents. But he thought that as long as he was stuck waiting, he might as well attempt to accomplish *something*.

So he decided to try to get the suspect to implicate himself.

"So," he said, turning to Matt, "you must have a lot of experience mixing chemicals and dangerous compounds, huh?"

"What makes you say that?"

Nick nodded at the canisters on the high shelf.

"Ka-blam?"

"Oh, that," Matt said, chuckling. If he were panicked about having left his itching powder in plain sight, he sure didn't show it. "That's not hard to make. You could do it yourself with some—"

"What's the stuff in the little container on the end?" Silas said, interrupting. "The one without a label?"

Nick was torn between the urge to put his face in his hands and the desire to wrap his hands around Silas's neck. Somehow, he managed to resist both and keep his gaze trained on Matt.

The guy sure didn't look panicked, not exactly, but his face did flush a deep shade of pink.

"That's just ... umm ... titanium shavings," Matt said. "We throw some in when we want an explosion to be especially sparkly. Like in fireworks. Of course, we don't use them as much as we used to. Why blow something up for real when you can do it with a computer?"

It was an obvious attempt to change the subject. And with Silas around, it worked.

"Because a real explosion is cooler!" Silas proclaimed.

"I couldn't agree more," Matt said.

"Computer animation always looks so computery! And animated!"

"You're preaching to the choir," Matt said. And then he and Silas shared a high-five.

"But real stuff blowing up . . . what's not to love?"

"Amen, brother."

And on it went.

All the while, Nick was thinking: *He's lying. Titanium shavings aren't orange-brown. They're silver.*

"So what's the deal with all the CGI on this movie?" Silas said when he and Matt were through singing the praises of blowing up real stuff. "Cash usually doesn't use it in his movies at all."

"Cash has never had a budget like this before," said Matt. He shook his head and sighed before adding, in a mumble, "Or a star like this."

"What's wrong with the star?" Silas asked.

"Yeah," Nick said, suddenly interested again in

the conversation. "Why would anyone want to slip itching powder into Mr. Wilder's costume?"

"I'm not convinced anyone did," Matt said. "It's not like Damon needed a reason to flip out. Since day one of shooting, he's been . . . well, let's just say this has been an interesting show to work on."

Silas furrowed his brow.

"Show? I thought this was a movie."

"It is," Matt said. "When you're in the business, everything you shoot is called a show, whether it's a feature film or reality TV."

"Ohhhh," Silas said, looking like he was jotting this information in a mental notebook so that he'd remember to throw the phrase around later.

"So, Damon Wilder's been hard to work with?" Nick asked. He was determined to keep the topic from straying yet again.

Matt eyed him a moment.

"You're friends of Zoe Helms's nephew, right?" he said.

"That's right," said Nick.

"Then my answer is 'no comment.'"

Matt smiled to show that he didn't mean any offense, and then he turned to a nearby work bench.

He picked up a black box with an antennae and two small joysticks jutting out of it.

"Now, who wants to see a giant talking robot head?"

When Tesla and DeMarco reached the side street where the cars were parked, they found the protestors still clustered at the edge of the set. A different security guard—a woman this time—was keeping an eye on them. She looked profoundly bored.

"Hey, hey, ho, ho!" chanted the protestor whom Silas had dubbed "Smelly Spider-Man Fan."

"Damon Wilder's got to go!" came the reply from the rest of the group.

"Hey, hey, ho, ho!" Smelly Spider-Man Fan said again.

"Don't you have somewhere to go?" called out the security guard.

"Excuse me," DeMarco said to the guard. "We just need to get something from my aunt's car."

"Sure," said the guard. "You're with Miss Helms, right? You need to get yourselves set passes. And you probably shouldn't walk around without your aunt, even after you have 'em."

"Fascists!" Smelly Spider-Man Fan yelled from across the street.

The guard rolled her eyes.

"You go get the box," Tesla said to DeMarco. "I'm curious about something."

As DeMarco headed for his aunt's car, Tesla turned and walked up to the protestors.

"All right," she said to no one in particular, "what's the deal?"

"What do you mean?" asked Smelly Spider-Man Fan.

"What do you guys have against Damon Wilder?"

"Don't play dumb with us," said one of the other protestors. (His snarling tone reminded Tesla of what Silas had called him: "Rude Batman Fan.") "Just because you're *so special* that you get to go on set doesn't mean that we"—and here he motioned to the crowd—"the lowly rabble, are idiots."

"Hey, it just hit the 'Net last night," said the boy whom Silas had referred to as "Stellan Something" . . . or maybe it was his brother, Casey Something. "Maybe she really doesn't know."

"Yeah," Anime Girl said to Rude Batman Fan. "Geez, you don't always have to be such a jerk."

Rude Batman Fan crossed his arms across his chest and sulked.

"We can show you what the deal is," Stellan or Casey Something said to Tesla, smiling at her in a nervous but friendly sort of way. "Casey, use your phone."

So he was Stellan. That was one mystery solved. Casey, who looked to be fourteen or fifteen years old to his brother's eleven or twelve, pulled a cell phone from his pocket and turned it on.

"What's going on?" asked DeMarco, who had returned with the box of homemade movie props cradled in his arms.

"We're about to find out why hey, hey, ho, ho, Damon Wilder's got to go," Tesla said.

"That was one of mine," Stellan said with shy pride.

Casey called up an app and, after some quick thumb-typing, handed the phone to Tesla.

"The rumors started a few days ago," he said. "Then this showed up on YouTube."

A video began to play on the phone's screen. The

title of the video was *Damon Wilder Goes WILD!!!* The image was shaky and slightly grainy, but it was immediately recognizable.

The video had been shot not fifty yards away, on the street outside the Veranda Theater. Metalman, his armor scuffed and scraped, was talking to a pretty young woman in a lab coat as smoke swirled around them.

"I know you didn't want to do that, Metalman," the woman said. "But you had no choice. The zomboid fever had driven them insane."

"Here it comes," said Stellan.

"I blame myself," Metalman intoned in a stiff, emotionless voice. "It was I who brought Lord Computron to face earth justice. I who unwittingly allowed him to spread his evil here."

"Oh, man," DeMarco said, shaking his head.

Tesla didn't have to ask what he was talking about.

It was obviously Damon Wilder in the Metalman suit. And his performance was *horrible*. Tesla had seen more convincing acting in grade-school plays about meteorology and good nutrition.

The image on the cell phone kept shaking and

shifting, and for a split second a dark smudge could be seen in the upper-left corner:

A person's fingertip.

"We're not just watching this *on* a cell phone. It was also shot *with* a cell phone," Tesla said.

She looked over at DeMarco.

"So there's a spy on the set," he said.

Anime Girl said, "Keep watching. It gets better."

"By which she means worse," added Stellan.

On the screen, Metalman took a lurching step forward and then he clenched a fist and thumped it against his armored chest.

"A human heart still beats inside this metal shell," he said robotically. "And today that heart is breaking. Lord Computron has broken it. I have broken it. And there is only one thing that can—what do you think you're doing?"

Wilder's emotionless drone had suddenly disappeared. He sounded human again. And angry.

"I said *what* do you *think* you are *doing?*" he said, grating out the words.

"Checking the fog machine," said a man's voice off-screen. It sounded familiar.

"Checking the fog machine? *Checking the fog*

machine?!" was Wilder's incredulous reply. "In the middle of a scene?!?"

"I'm sorry, Damon," the man said. "The fog machine was about to— "

"Do I care what the fog machine was about to do? Do I? *Do I?*"

"Well—"

Wilder ripped off his Metalman helmet and hurled it with all his might at the man they couldn't see. There was a painful-sounding *thunk*, and several people could be heard gasping.

"I do not care about the fog machine!" Wilder said in a rage. His hair was slick with sweat, his eyes wide. "I care about stopping Lord Computron! I care about stopping the zomboid virus! I care about saving the human race! And I care about holding on to the last shreds of my own humanity! When I put on this costume, I'm not Damon Wilder, who has to worry about amateurs wandering around trashing his scenes! I am a hero who has to worry about protecting everyone and everything! Including my very soul!"

"Let's just take a minute," said another voice. This one belonged to Cash Ashkinos.

"I don't want to take a minute, Cash!" Wilder answered. "I just want to know that this idiot isn't going to go skipping right in front of me and ruin my scene!"

"I absolutely apologize, Damon."

Tesla didn't think Wilder could open his eyes any wider, yet somehow he managed to. They looked like a couple of pupil-pocked ping-pong balls about to pop right out of his face.

"What did I just say, Matt?" he roared. "I'm not Damon! I . . . am . . . Metalman!"

"Hey—that's Matt Gore!" said DeMarco.

And that's a motive, thought Tesla.

"If Damon Wilder had done that to *me*," DeMarco said as he carried the box of special effects gadgets back to Matt's trailer, "I would've put something a lot worse than itching powder down his back."

"What could've been worse than itching powder?" asked Tesla.

DeMarco looked at her sadly.

"Tez," he said, "remember who my sisters are.

I've found stuff worse than itching powder on my toothbrush. I've found stuff worse than itching powder in my shorts. I've found stuff worse than itching powder stuffed up my—"

"Okay, okay. I get it."

The kids had been through the set enough times already that they were now a familiar sight; most crew members simply ignored them. But one—a husky man in a flannel shirt, jeans, and heavy work boots—suddenly stepped into their path, blocking their way.

"Whoa, there," he said. "You two look a little young to be Teamsters."

"Uhh, that's because we're not," Tesla said.

"Whatever those are," added DeMarco.

"Teamsters," the man said, "transport and assemble film equipment. And their union makes sure that they, and *only they*, do the transporting and assembling. Which makes me wonder who's got you doing that."

He pointed a stubby, callous-tipped finger at the cardboard box in DeMarco's arms.

"We were going to show it to Matt, the special effects guy," DeMarco said.

"Matt Gore's hiring ten-year-old assistants?"

"I'm eleven," muttered Tesla.

"I'm twelve," grumbled DeMarco.

"And anyway," Tesla said, "we're not Matt Gore's assistants. We're guests."

Tesla looked pointedly at DeMarco.

"Zoe Helms is my aunt," he told the man.

"Ohhhhh. Zoe Helms is your auuuuuuuunt," the man said, sneering in a *la-di-da* kind of way. "Well, you know what, kid? Usually, it wouldn't matter if George Lucas was your uncle, Michael Bay was your cousin, and Walt Disney was your long-lost twin. Unattended children cannot go wandering around an active set. But I happen to like Zoe, so I'm going to cut her some slack and let it slide. This time."

The man reached out with a big hand and patted DeMarco on the head.

"Don't make me regret it, *nephew*. Now go to wherever you're supposed to be, and stay there."

The Teamster guy walked away whistling.

"Come on," Tesla said to DeMarco. "We need to hurry and get back. Leaving Silas with our prime suspect makes me nervous."

"Don't worry. Nick's there to keep him out of

trouble," DeMarco said. "What could possibly go wrong?"

"How dare you meddle in my affairs, Silas Kuskie?" a voice suddenly boomed from somewhere nearby. "I shall commit what crimes I like . . . and kill *whom* I like! Starting with you!"

Tesla and DeMarco burst into a sprint.

They both knew that voice.

It belonged to Matt Gore!

"Die! Die! Die!" he bellowed.

Tesla and DeMarco tore around one truck, dashed past another, and then went pounding up the ramp into the special effects trailer. There they found Nick and Silas staring slack-jawed at the fiend who was roaring threats at them:

Lord Computron.

Specifically, Lord Computron's robot head.

Silas glanced over his shoulder and grinned.

"Cool, huh?" he said, not noticing that Tesla and DeMarco were flushed and panting. He turned back to Lord Computron's giant disembodied head.

Its glowing eyes were shifting this way and that, and its mouth moved when Matt—who was standing in the corner holding the control pad—hollered out the words.

"Feel the deadly sting of my laser vision!"

Then Matt pushed a button, and the light in Lord Computron's eyes shone from yellow to bright red.

Then the right eye flared white and, with a pop and a puff of smoke, burned out.

"Oh, well," Matt said with a sigh. "Not using CGI does have its downside."

He pushed another button, and the giant head powered down and went still.

"Who cares about downsides?" Silas pointed at the robot head. "That. Is. Cool. Cash should be making the whole movie with stuff like that."

Matt shook his head sadly.

"Movie fans these days expect CGI. And doing effects with a computer gives the studio more control. If they think the audience wants exploding unicorns? Type-type, click-click—you've got exploding unicorns. Shooting with practical effects—the kind you actually do live on set with props like this one—that's too slow, too old-fashioned. No one's interested in *building* things anymore. Not when you can fake it with a few mouse clicks."

"You're wrong about that," Tesla said. She looked

over at DeMarco and waved him forward. "Go ahead. Show him."

"We built these for the film I'm directing," Silas said as DeMarco brought the box of props to Matt. "And writing. And producing. And editing and scoring, too, once it's ready."

Matt leaned over the box, gazed into it for a moment, and then reached down toward the grappling hook and wrist launcher that Nick and Tesla had built for Bald Eagle.

Perfect, Tesla thought.

Except that Matt was simply moving the grappling hook and launcher to the side so that he could get at the one thing Tesla didn't want him to pull out: the robo-arm. *Not* perfect!

"Interesting," Matt said.

As he examined the robo-arm, made mostly of ice-pop sticks and zip ties, it looked rickety and fragile. All he had to do was hold it the wrong way or grip it too hard, and the whole thing would crumple into splinters, putty, and string.

Matt found the handle, took hold of it, and gave it a tug.

The "fingers" curled in on themselves, making

an ice-pop fist.

Matt looked up at the kids—and then he burst into a huge grin.

"I love it!" he said. "You guys are naturals. What else you got in here?"

He carefully put the robo-arm back in the box, laying it beside the grappling hook and the launcher, before pulling out the homemade camera-steadier contraption.

"Whoa. What the heck is this?"

"Show him how it works, DeMarco," Tesla said.

"Sure." DeMarco handed the prop box to Nick and then took the camera steadier from Matt's hands, moving closer to Lord Computron. "Now, Mr. Gore. Why don't you come over this way and look at it like this?"

Matt moved forward.

Nick stepped back, blocking Matt's view of the box.

With Matt facing the other direction, Tesla snatched the robo-arm and shoved it at Silas.

Silas stared back at her blankly.

Silas was the tallest of the four kids, but, unfortunately, he wasn't the most devious. He hadn't intuitively grasped the plan—or even noticed that there was one.

"Let's say we want to start with a close-up of Lord Computron," DeMarco was saying. "Well, we'd just set up right here and—"

"Hey—I see it now! It's a homemade Steadicam!" Matt said. He started to turn to face the others. "Which one of you dreamed up this little—?"

"It was me! All me!" DeMarco said quickly. "And just look at how well it works! Up, down, this way, that way, and the camera mount never wobbles. You want to try it?"

"Well, I—"

"Here, take it. See how that feels?"

DeMarco looked over Matt's shoulder long enough to throw his friends a glare that said, *Hurry up!*

Tesla jabbed a finger at Silas three times. *Point point point. You.*

Again, Silas stared at her blankly.

Then she jabbed the finger at the robo-arm three times. *Point point point. The robo-arm.*

Silas still stared at her blankly.

Then she jabbed the finger at the high shelf holding the powder. *Point point point. The powder!*

At last, Silas stopped staring at her blankly. Understanding finally dawned in his eyes.

He grinned, gave Tesla and Nick a double-thumbs-up, and took the robo-arm, tiptoeing toward the shelf.

When he was close enough, Silas reached up with the robo-arm, groped around for the right canister, pulled back the lever that curled the fingers, and proceeded very slowly to take down the jar marked KA-BLAM!

When Silas turned to face Nick and Tesla, he was beaming with pride. The look of horror on his friends' faces was completely mystifying. He had no idea that, over his head, he was holding the wrong canister.

Or that the canister, marked KA-BLAM! in big, thick, explode-y letters, was starting to slip through the robo-arm's clumsy wooden fingers.

Both Nick and Tesla began vigorously shaking their heads while also stabbing their pointer fingers up at the shelf.

Point point point. Point point point.

Put it back! Put it back!

Silas gave them a stare that was meant to say, *Geez, make up your minds. You just told me to take it down!*

The canister slipped an inch, then another inch. Then six more.

"Okay. I see. Very clever," Matt was saying as DeMarco kept trying new ways to keep him interested in the camera steadier. "So, what else do you have in your box of—?"

"Hold on!" DeMarco said a little too eagerly. "You haven't seen the *really* cool part yet."

"Oh?"

"Yeah! Uhhh . . ."

An awkward silence filled the room while De-Marco tried to figure out what the "really cool part" was.

Silas, meanwhile, gave an irritated shrug before turning to put the KA-BLAM canister back on the shelf.

He was still holding the can over his head, however, and his shrugging caused it to slip even more. Now, the only thing that the robo-arm fingers were gripping was the lid. And if the can did fall, well, it was going to land right on Silas's head.

". . . pennies!" DeMarco was saying. "You use pennies for weights. So it also doubles as a piggy bank!"

Nick and Tesla liked explosions as much as the next kid, but when the thing exploding was their friend's head—and maybe them along with it—well, then, not so much.

Tesla reflexively shut her eyes.

Nick kept his eyes open, but only because he was concentrating all of his effort on not yelling.

Finally, the canister fell.

Fortunately, by then Silas was holding it over its old spot on the shelf, so the drop was mere millimeters. It landed silently, without even a clunk. And, more important, without a *KA-BLAM!*

Nick breathed a sigh of relief.

Then Silas turned toward Nick. In the process, he knocked the robo-hand against the container of orange-brown powder, the one he was *supposed* to have grabbed in the first place.

It went flying.

And so did Nick. He dove forward, caught the container when it was barely a foot off the floor, and then landed on top of it, sprawled out like a squashed bug.

"Whoa! Are you okay?" Matt said, taking a step toward his friend's prone body.

"I'm fine! No problem!" Nick said as he scrambled to his feet. "I just, uhh, fell down."

"He does that a lot," Tesla said.

Nick managed to slide the container behind his back as he turned around to face Matt. He found the man staring back at him quizzically.

An icy chill ran down Nick's spine.

They'd been caught! What was Matt going to do?

But then Nick noticed that Matt wasn't staring at him. He was staring at somebody behind him. Namely, Silas.

Who was still holding the robo-arm.

Over his head.

Surely Matt could see that Silas had grabbed something off the shelf. Nick braced himself to make a mad dash out of the trailer.

But then Silas said: "Cool bonus feature with this—it makes a great back scratcher." And then he began rubbing the fingers against his back. A couple pop sticks snapped off and fell to the floor, but Matt didn't seem to notice.

"Well," Tesla said suddenly, "you've been extremely generous with your time, Mr. Gore, and we know you're a busy man. So we should probably be toddling along."

"Yes," agreed Nick. "Definitely time to toddle." Although he was thinking: *Toddle? Is that a word?* But there was no time to figure that out, because at any moment Matt would start wondering what Nick was holding behind his back.

"Bye!" Nick said as he sidled away, keeping his

face turned to Matt the whole while.

"Bye!" said Tesla and Silas and DeMarco as they, too, moved toward the ramp leading out of the trailer.

Matt looked a little disappointed to see them go.

"Thanks for showing me your special effects stuff, you guys," he said. "Tell Zoe to bring you back when we blow up Lord Computron."

"Totally! Will do! Can't wait!" said Nick.

"Whew," Nick added. But not until they had safely left the trailer and were on the other side of a nearby van, well out of earshot.

When all four had found a sheltered spot between two trailers, they sat on the ground in a circle and Nick brought out the plastic container.

Silas tossed the robo-arm back in the box of props DeMarco was holding.

"So, what is that?" Silas said.

"Proof," DeMarco said.

Silas stared at it.

"Some Tupperware full of sand is proof?"

"Not sand," said DeMarco. "Itching powder."

"Maybe," Nick said. He set the container down, took hold of the rubbery lid, and slowly and ever so gently peeled it back.

All four kids leaned in to peer down at the granular, pumpkin-colored substance inside.

"Still looks like sand to me," Silas said.

"From an orange beach?" said DeMarco.

"I'm sure there are orange beaches."

"Where?"

"Somewhere."

"Why keep sand from one on your shelf?"

Silas shrugged. "Because it's pretty?"

DeMarco shook his head. "It's not sand," he muttered.

Nick looked over at his sister.

"But is it itching powder?"

"Well, it doesn't look exactly like the kind I made," Tesla said. "It's smoother. Finer. And the color's not quite—hey!"

DeMarco had snatched the container away from Nick and stalked off a few paces.

"I'll tell you if it's itching powder right now."

"No, DeMarco!" Tesla cried.

"Don't do it!" said Nick.

But it was too late. DeMarco was already tilting the container to pour some of its contents onto the back of his left hand. Once he had a little heap of the orange-brown powder on his skin, he straightened the container and waited.

"Does it itch?" asked Nick.

"No."

"Does it burn?" asked Silas.

"No."

"Does it tingle?" asked Tesla.

"No. It doesn't do anything." DeMarco brought his left hand up to his face and sniffed. "Except smell like Tang."

"Tang?" said Nick.

"Yeah. It's got that sweet fake-citrus smell. Like Tang or Kool-Aid."

"Really?" said Silas.

He walked over to DeMarco, licked the tip of an index finger, and then plunged it into the container. When he pulled it out, his fingertip was coated in orange-brown powder.

Silas was about to stick the finger in his mouth when Nick grabbed his arm to stop him. "Come on!" Nick said with a groan. "Can we *please* be more careful with unknown substances?"

"It's not unknown," said Silas. "I know exactly what it is."

"What is it?" said Tesla.

Silas raised his powdered finger to his nose and sniffed. Then he handed the jar to Nick and brushed the powder off his finger. "Oh, yeah. No doubt about it," he said. "It's Metamucil."

"Meta-*what*?" said DeMarco.

Silas nodded. "I'd know that smell anywhere. My granddad takes it three times a day. Mixes it up in a big glass of water and guzzles it down."

"Why?" DeMarco said. "What does it do?"

Silas shot Tesla an uncomfortable look.

"There's a lady present," he said.

Tesla glowered at him.

"I have a granddad, too," she said. "I know what Metamucil is."

"Well, I still don't," DeMarco said.

Silas stepped closer and whispered in his ear.

"Ew," DeMarco said. He put the container on the ground and backed away. "Okay. Enough. I get it."

Silas stepped away, too.

"Boy," DeMarco said. "Getting old stinks."

"No kidding," said Silas.

Nick picked up the container and started walking back toward the special effects trailer.

"Where are you going?" Tesla said.

"I'm gonna leave this where Matt can find it," Nick said. "He seems like a nice guy, and I don't want him having trouble with his, you know, because of us."

"All right. But be careful. Just because that wasn't the itching powder doesn't mean Matt's not the culprit."

Nick nodded and then crept off.

"'The culprit,'" Silas said with a giggle. "I love it when Tez talks like that."

Tesla silenced him with a glare.

Nick returned a moment later. "Hey, guys," he said. "I think I saw—"

"There they are!" blared a familiar high-pitched voice.

"Yeah!" an even higher-pitched voice chimed in. "There they are!"

Elesha and Monique came around one of the nearby trailers and pointed at their brother and his friends.

Aunt Zoe stepped out behind them.

"I am *very* disappointed in you, young man," she said. "I bring you onto an active film set as my guest—under extremely trying circumstances—and you repay me by wandering off as if this was your private playground?"

"I'm sorry," DeMarco said, his head hanging low.

Elesha and Monique beamed.

"I told you we could find them," Elesha said.

"Yeah, we told you we could find them," Monique added.

"All right, girls," Aunt Zoe said.

"DeMarco was trying to help you," Tesla said to Aunt Zoe. "It's obvious something strange is going on around here, and we're actually pretty good at figuring out—"

"You," Aunt Zoe said. "Come here."

She wasn't looking at Tesla.

It was the production assistant they had seen at the beginning of the day, the young woman in the ASK ME ABOUT MY SCREENPLAY T-shirt. She carried a huge Starbucks cup in each hand.

"Yes, Ms. Helms?"

"Abby, I need you to take these children home

immediately," Zoe said.

"What?" said Tesla and Nick.

"No!" said DeMarco.

"Oh, come on," said Silas.

"But I have to bring Damon his triple venti no foam soy latte," Abby said. "And Mr. Ashkinos is waiting for his grande quad nonfat no-whip one-pump mocha. Then I have to pick up Mr. Ortmann's dry cleaning and get more pretzels for the craft service table and hand out the call sheets for tomorrow's shoot and—"

"I understand, Abby," Aunt Zoe said. "I started out as a P.A., too."

Abby smiled.

Aunt Zoe reached out and took the coffee cups.

"I'll deliver these," she said. "The rest can wait."

Abby's smile faded.

"Yes, Ms. Helms."

Aunt Zoe turned and started walking away.

"The one in your right hand is the triple venti no foam soy latte!" Abby called after her. "Whatever you do, don't give Damon the grande quad nonfat no-whip one-pump mocha!"

"Got it!" Aunt Zoe called back. "Now, go!"

When she was gone, Abby heaved a tremendous sigh. "Show biz," she said sadly.

"So," Silas said as Abby herded them all off, "have you written a screenplay?"

Abby's smile returned.

"Funny you should ask," she said. "Let me tell you about it . . ."

". . . then, with a final tortured scream, the last of the bear-dragons crashes into the burning castle, sending shards of stone and flaming fur flying in all directions," Abby was saying. "Cut to: Goldilocks and Prince Brock watching from the top of Mt. Destiny. Goldilocks, lowering her bow: 'Your palace is gone, Brock. But at least you know that all in your kingdom are finally free to live in peace.' Prince Brock, gazing worshipfully at the mighty she-warrior: 'And free to love, my lady. And free to love.' They kiss. Fade to black. Roll credits."

In the backseat of Abby's ancient Toyota sedan, Silas slowly clapped his hands together once, twice, three times, four times, five times, the pace and intensity building until he was applauding with all his might.

No one joined in, but he didn't seem to notice.

Monique and Elesha, who were squeezed together in the front passenger seat, just looked at each other and grimaced.

"Can we get out now?" said Tesla, who was squeezed so tightly between Silas and DeMarco that she could barely breathe.

They'd been sitting in the driveway in front of Silas's house for an extra ten minutes so that Abby could finish describing her script.

Nick opened the door he was squished up against, and he and DeMarco spilled out onto the pavement. Tesla scrambled out after them, and then Monique and Elesha hopped out, too.

Yet Silas lingered behind to tell Abby to stick with it. He said he was certain it was only a matter of time before one of the studios snatched up *Goldilocks Rises*.

"See ya at the Oscars," Silas said before sliding out of the car with the box of props.

He put down the box and gave Abby two thumbs-up as she backed out of the driveway and puttered off.

"That is a surefire blockbuster," he said.

"That story was nothing but sword fights and monsters," countered Elesha.

"Exactly," Silas said. "Surefire. Blockbuster."

"So . . . what now?" DeMarco asked.

"What do you think?" said Tesla.

DeMarco nodded.

"Right."

Tesla didn't even have to say it.

They were going back.

"What about you know who?" Nick whispered.

He jerked his head at Elesha and Monique.

"We know you're talking about us," Elesha said.

"What?" said Monique, looking surprised. "Oh, I mean, yeah. We know you're talking about us!"

"You wanna go snoop some more, don't you?" said Elesha.

"Yes," Tesla said. "We want to go snoop some more."

Elesha crossed her arms over her chest and grinned an evil grin.

Monique copied her sister.

Elesha opened her mouth to speak, but Tesla interrupted her. "Before you run off to tell on us, you should know that your aunt's movie is in really big trouble. Which means that your aunt is in trouble. This was supposed to be her big break. Her shot at making huge Hollywood hits instead of cheesy straight-to-video action flicks."

"Hey! Cash Ashkinos's movies are not cheesy!" Silas said in protest. "They're—oh, okay, so they are cheesy. But in a good way!"

"But someone's trying to wreck your aunt's film," Tesla continued as if Silas hadn't spoken. "And that could wreck her career. As far as I can tell, we're the only ones trying to do something about it. So if you want to march off to your mother and tell her we got kicked off the set and ruin any chance we have of going back and helping your aunt, fine. You go right ahead. But when Aunt Zoe is producing TV commercials for the local car wash instead of making blockbuster movies because *you* let somebody sabotage *Metalman*, I hope you'll have the common decency to at least tell her you're sorry."

"Ha!" Elesha barked. "Nice try at a guilt trip, but we're not falling for it."

She turned and started to stomp off toward the

house.

She stopped when she realized that nobody was walking with her.

"We're not falling for it," Elesha repeated. She looked back and saw that not only did Monique not echo her, she wasn't following her, either. Monique was still standing in front of Tesla and the others.

"What's the matter?" Elesha said to Monique.

"Well . . ." Monique kicked at a pebble and started to speak again, but then snapped her mouth shut.

"Don't you think that," she began, hesitant, "maybe, just maybe, couldn't she be . . . the slightest little bit, well . . . ?"

"Couldn't she be *what*?" Elesha snapped.

"Right?" Monique said. "Because if she is and we don't let them go back and Metalman is ruined and Aunt Zoe can't make movies anymore, maybe it will kind of be our fault."

Elesha gasped.

DeMarco and Silas gasped.

Nick and Tesla gasped.

None of them saw it coming: the answer to a mystery that had baffled the neighborhood long before Nick and Tesla had ever arrived in Half Moon Bay.

One of the Davison girls *was* indeed capable of feeling something other than spite.

But were both?

Elesha stared at her sister in shock. Then, slowly, almost imperceptibly at first, her expression changed. The surprise morphed into something else.

Nick was hoping for goodwill tinged with remorse for past slights.

He got a sly smirk instead.

"All right. We'll give them their chance to save the day," Elesha said. "For a price."

Monique instantly forgot about feeling something other than spite.

"Yeah," she said, copying her sister's smirk. "For a price."

"Name it," said Tesla.

"Name it, she says," DeMarco grumbled as Elesha and Monique walked away half a minute later. "It's a deal, she says. Haven't you ever heard of negotiating, Tez?"

Tesla shrugged.

"We don't have time to negotiate."

"That's easy for you to say. You're not the one who just agreed to do all of your sisters' chores for the next six months!"

Tesla put a hand on DeMarco's shoulder.

"You're a wonderful nephew," she said.

DeMarco took a deep breath.

"Yes," he said, sighing heavily. "I am."

Nick put up a hand as if asking to be called on in class.

"Hey, guys? Aren't you forgetting something? Elesha and Monique aren't the only reason we're going to have trouble getting back on to that set. We're still going to have to slip past the guards and P.A.s."

"Thanks for the reminder, Mr. Worst-Case Scenario," Tesla said.

Nick lowered his hand, looking satisfied.

"That's what I'm here for."

"In a situation like this, there's one question we should be asking ourselves," Silas pontificated. "W.W.B.E.D.?"

"'Wuhbed'?" Tesla said.

Silas shook his head.

"No, no, no. What Would Bald Eagle Do?"

Nick grinned.

"Silas, you are truly a visionary," he said.

"He is?" said Tesla.

"Yeah," said DeMarco. "He is?"

Silas looked slightly offended by his friends' obvious skepticism.

"He is," Nick said, "because we *can* get Bald Eagle to help us."

"That might be a little tough, considering that he doesn't exist," said Tesla.

Nick's grin grew larger.

"He doesn't?"

He let his eyes slide, slide, slide slowly to the right.

The others followed his gaze . . . and found themselves looking at a feathered figure that, hours earlier, had been left propped up against a tree in DeMarco's yard. The stunt dummy!

Tesla smiled approvingly at her brother and, without even knowing it, quoted a line she'd heard in a dozen movies.

"You know, it's so crazy that it just might work."

NEARLY HUMAN HOMEMADE STUNT DUMMY

THE STUFF

- Pair of sweatpants or pajama bottoms

- Hoodie

- Old towels, dishtowels, wash cloths, small blankets, pillows of various sizes, and anything else that will make good stuffing

- Several plastic grocery bags

- Socks (one pair for the dummy's feet, plus extras to use as stuffing)

- Gloves

- Lots of duct tape

- Optional: ¾-inch PVC pipes and joints

NOTE: The materials for this project depend on the size of the stunt dummy you want to make. Since a stunt dummy's job is to take the place of an actor during dangerous stunts, you should construct your version with clothing that's roughly the same size as your actor (or, even better, one size smaller, to make it easier to put costumes on it!). Sweatpants or pajamas are good for the dummy's legs because they have no pockets or belt loops that get snagged on things. A hoodie is a must—you will use the hood to create the dummy's head. (Unless your movie involves a headless monster, in which case, no head.) Visit a thrift shop to buy the dummy's clothing. While there, also get old towels, pillows, and small blankets for the stuffing.

THE SETUP

1. Start by laying out the dummy's shirt and pants. Doing so will help you estimate how much stuffing—towels, pillows, etc.—you'll need.

2. Build the arms. Choose four towels (or blankets), each as long as the sleeves of the hoodie. Roll each towel length-wise and then bend it in half. Wind duct tape around each towel to keep it rolled. Pack the towels into the shirt-sleeves, two per sleeve, with one towel forming the upper arm and one forming the forearm. (For stiffer arms, fill the entire sleeve with one long, folded towel or blanket.) Add smaller towels, blankets, etc., to give the arms a natural shape. You want the stuffing to be packed tightly so that it will stay in place when the dummy gets knocked around. Leave some room in the elbow area so that the arms will bend.

3. To build the legs, repeat step 2, filling the pants with two folded towels per leg. Add more stuffing as needed.

4. Fill the torso. Group pillows and other stuffing material to form the chest and stomach. It's best to use a few large pillows instead of many smaller ones so that the dummy's torso will move like a single, solid mass. Wrap duct tape around the pillows to hold them together, and slip them into the hoodie. Fill in any empty space as needed to create a natural shape and keep everything packed tight.

5. Create the head. Stuff the hood with one or more balled-up towels or blankets. (If you have a sports ball that's the right size, you can use that to help create a rounded shape). Pull the hood down to cover the stuffing, and wrap tape around the hood.

THE FINAL STEPS

---

1. Stuff the socks with dishtowels, other socks, and whatever other materials are on hand to form the feet of the dummy. Attach to the pants with duct tape.

2. Stuff the gloves with plastic grocery bags, torn-up paper, or anything else that can fit into the fingers easily. Attach to the sleeves of the hoodie with duct tape.

3. Join the torso to the waist, tucking the waist of the hoodie into the pants, and tape in place. (If your dummy will be flying around, use large safety pins to keep the torso and waist securely attached.) Your stunt dummy is ready for action!

Here are some additional tips:

- Dress the dummy in the same clothes worn by the actor. To avoid having to share clothes between the dummy and the actor, go to a thrift store and buy two sets of similar clothing (for example jeans and a plain sweatshirt).

- Use a hat, wig, sunglasses, and/or additional hood to conceal the dummy's head and face.

- When filming your stunt dummy, remember that less is more. Even though people will know you didn't really drop a person off a roof, the scene will be more fun for your audience if it isn't too obvious that you're using a stunt dummy. Film from a distance, keep the dummy in motion, or hide it partially in shadows or by scenery. When you edit the scenes of your movie, it's better to switch back and forth quickly between the dummy (far away) and an actor (close up) than to have a single, prolonged shot of the dummy.

If you want your stunt dummy to be stiffer and easier to pose, try making a "skeleton" out of ¾-inch PVC pipe (you can use pieces left over from building your camera rig, page 25). You may need an adult to cut the pipe. Wrap the pipe in towels, slip each segment into place, and then connect the pieces. Depending on which types of PVC connectors you use, you can position the dummy with bent arms or legs, sitting down, etc.

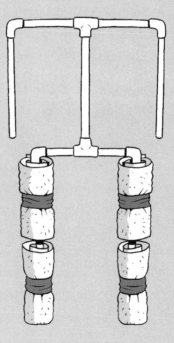

Nick and Tesla ran to Uncle Newt's house to get their bicycles. Silas and DeMarco would meet them there, bringing the dummy, props, and other materials they'd need to complete phase two of their plan. Then, together, they would bike back downtown to the movie set.

"See ya in a minute," Nick said when he and Tesla reached the driveway. "I've gotta go to the bathroom."

He swerved toward the front door.

Tesla gave him thirty seconds before following him into the house.

She found him where she knew she would: sitting on the floor in their room, hunched over the laptop. He was pounding on the keyboard and double-clicking icons, but nothing happened. The computer was still frozen.

"So, you had to go to the bathroom, huh?" Tesla said.

"Yes, and I still do," said Nick. "I just thought I'd check on the computer first."

"All right. You've checked." Tesla bent down and shut the laptop. "Now, come on. There'll be plenty of time to read crackpot theories later. We've got a real problem to solve first."

"We already *had* a real problem. You don't have to keep finding us even *more*. I mean, geez, Tez. Sometimes I think you'd rather get in trouble with Silas and DeMarco than try to find Mom and Dad with me."

Tesla winced.

Nick did, too.

"That was harsh," Tesla said.

"I know," said Nick. "I'm sorry."

They stood for a moment in silence, not looking at each other.

"Maybe you're right, though," Tesla said finally. "A little bit."

"What do you mean?"

"Well, it's not that I don't want to find Mom and Dad. I do. It's just . . . I don't know. Maybe I'm afraid they're mixed up in something that's too big for us. Too grown-up. Maybe I'm afraid of failing."

"You haven't been afraid to go after kidnappers and thieves and spies and saboteurs."

"But that felt different. Almost like it was . . ."

Tesla struggled to find the right word.

When she finally thought of it, she surprised Nick with a smile.

"Practice," she said.

Nick smiled back at her.

"Practice. I like that. And when we've had enough practice . . . ?"

"Then nothing is going to keep us from finding Mom and Dad. Absolutely nothing."

Tesla reached out and put a hand on her brother's shoulder.

"I promise," she said.

A couple minutes later, when Nick and Tesla came down the driveway with their bikes, they found De-Marco and Silas waiting for them. DeMarco had a backpack slung on his back. Silas had a superhero slung on his back. It was Bald Eagle, of course. Or at least his stunt-dummy double, decked out in a feathered costume.

"Are you going to make it to the set like that?" Nick said. "That thing's kinda heavy."

"Aw, this is nothin'," Silas said. "I once rode my bike three miles down the Pacific Coast Highway and back again carrying an old fax machine, two pounds of flour, and DeMarco."

Nick gave DeMarco a quizzical look.

DeMarco shrugged. "It was a dare," he said. "You had to be there."

"Enough gab," said Silas. "Let's get going before—"

"Hey, kids," a voice called. "What ya up to?"

All four of them turned toward the house.

Uncle Newt was stepping out onto the front porch. As usual, he was wearing a smudge-covered lab coat over a tattered T-shirt and jeans. His wild graying hair was blackened with soot on one side, and his glasses were tilted across his long face at a

thirty-degree angle. In his right hand was a mug. In his left hand was a half-eaten Hot Pocket.

Also, he was on fire.

Or at least his lab coat was. The fabric on the lower-right side was smoldering and smoking.

"Mr. Holt!" Silas cried. "Stop, drop, and roll!"

"Not to be a stickler, Shiloh," Uncle Newt said, "but it's *Dr.* Holt, actually. Physics PhD from Stanford, engineering systems PhD from M.I.T. Oh, and there's my ethnomusicology PhD from Cal Berkeley, but I usually don't bring that one up. I mean, what was I thinking? Three years in the jungles of Borneo to master tribal drumming, and then I turn in my dissertation and never touch a bongo again."

While Uncle Newt was speaking, Tesla walked over to him, took the mug from his hand, and poured the cola in it onto the smoking coat.

There was a sizzle, and the smoldering stopped.

Tesla handed the mug back to her uncle.

"Oh. Right. On fire," he said. "Thank you."

"You're welcome," said Tesla.

She headed back toward her bike, which was lying on its side in the driveway.

Uncle Newt turned to Silas.

"So, Sidney," he said, "did you know that you have a giant man-owl on your back?"

"Yup," said Silas.

Uncle Newt brought his mug to his lips and started to take a sip. When no liquid reached his lips, he remembered that his niece had just used his beverage to extinguish a fire.

"All right," he said to Silas. "Well, enjoy."

And with that Uncle Newt started to head back into the house.

"Shouldn't we tell him what's going on?" Nick

whispered.

Tesla thought it over.

"Sure, why not." she finally said. "Hey, Uncle Newt! We're going downtown to try to catch some sneaky jerk who's been ruining DeMarco's aunt's movie by leaking embarrassing videos and putting itching powder in the star's costume!"

"Be back in time for breakfast," Uncle Newt replied without looking back. "Er—I mean, dinner."

And then he stepped back inside and closed the front door.

"Is there *anything* your uncle won't let you do?" Silas asked in awe.

"Sure," said Tesla. "Watch reality television."

"He also won't let me wash out the dirty beakers in his lab because he's been doing a lot of experiments with sodium lately, and water could trigger an exothermic reaction," said Nick.

Silas furrowed his brow.

"Trigger a what?"

"A ka-blam," Tesla offered as an explanation.

"Oh."

"Hey, guys?" DeMarco said. "I hate to interrupt this *fascinating* conversation, but don't we have a sneaky jerk to catch?"

"Right," said Tesla. "Let's roll!"

And the four friends—and one dummy—took off on their bikes and zipped up the street.

Across the street from the movie theater, the small group of protestors had shrunk even smaller. The only people left were the brothers, Stellan and Casey, plus their friend, the girl dressed as a pirate cat (a.k.a. Captain Bloodwhiskers). She was chanting: "Five-six-seven-eight, who do we hate-hate-hate? Daaaaaaaaaaaaaamon Wilder!"

"Meh," said Stellan. "Seems a little mean."

Casey shrugged.

"Fine," said Captain Bloodwhiskers. "We'll go back to 'We want a superhero, not a superzero.'"

"I'm tired of that one," said Stellan.

"I'm tired of all of them," grumbled Casey.

Stellan gave his older brother a "me, too" look. Metalman was their favorite comic book character, but it was getting harder and harder to believe they could make his next movie any better by standing around chanting slogans for the benefit of a solitary, bored-looking security guard.

"One-two-three-four!" the guard called to them from across the street. "Get a life!"

"Hey," Captain Bloodwhiskers said. "Look over there, Stellan. Your girlfriend's back."

"My what?" Stellan said as he turned in the direction she indicated. The girl was pointing at an alleyway across the street, just up the block from where the bored security guard was sitting and working on a Sudoku puzzle book. Stellan could see Tesla standing in front of the alley; behind her were Nick, Silas, and DeMarco.

She was gesturing for him to come over.

"That's Silas Kuskie and DeMarco Davison and those other two kids they were with this morning," Casey said. "I wonder what they want."

As they watched, Tesla placed a straightened index finger to her lips. *Shhhh.*

She then brought up her other index finger and curled it three times. *Come here.*

Stellan got the message. He looked at his brother, who gave a disinterested shrug, and then walked across the street.

"Hi," Tesla said once Stellan reached the alleyway.

"Hi," he said. Then Stellan noticed a feathered something-or-other piled on the ground farther up the alley. "Is that a dead turkey?"

"No," said Nick. "It's a stunt dummy in a superhero costume."

Stellan's eyes widened. "Whoa! Did you steal that from the set?"

"No, it's not from the set," Tesla said. "We've been kicked off the set, actually."

"Why?" Stellan said.

Silas opened his mouth to answer. Tesla slapped a hand over it.

"It's a long story that we don't have time to go into right now," she said. "The important thing is that we have to get back on the set. And we'd like you and your friends to help us."

"How?" said Stellan. "I mean, why should we?"

Tesla smiled at him.

"Because you guys hate this movie," she said, "and if the people making it don't want us back on the set, then we must be doing something that's going to get in the way of the movie, which is something you want, right?"

Stellan frowned. "I don't know if that makes sense."

"Me, neither," Silas said, causing DeMarco to thump him on the back of the head.

"Think of it like this," Nick said. "The enemy of my enemy is my friend."

"Yeah, well . . ." Stellan said, "suppose you do get back on the set. What exactly are you going to do?"

"Like I said, long story, no time," Tesla said. "You saw us walk onto the set with DeMarco's aunt earlier, so you know that part's real. Now, you have to decide: are you in or not?"

"Well . . ."

"Time," Tesla said, tapping an imaginary watch on her wrist. "We have none. In or out?"

"Okay, okay," Stellan said quickly. "What do we have to do?"

Tesla beamed a warm smile. But then her smile turned sly and wily.

"Trust me. You're gonna like this," she said. "You see that parking garage over there? Well . . ."

Dalasia Hewitt, the Sudoku-solving security guard, was bored. Only a single protestor was left across the street—the pirate-cat girl—and even she had stopped chanting and now just stood there talking on her cell phone. Dalasia had solved all the puzzles in her Sudoku book, and her shift would not be over for a few more hours. So when some sort of commotion seemed to be happening on top of the parking garage that sat catty-corner to the movie theater, she was quick to get out of her chair to check it out.

The garage should have been deserted; the production company had secured filming permits that let them close the street to all traffic. Yet Dalasia noticed some movement on one of the top floors. A dark silhouette appeared beside a shadow-draped concrete column.

"Look! He came!" the pirate-cat said, pointing at the garage. "It's Bald Eagle!"

"Who?" Dalasia said. She crossed the street to get a better look.

"Bald Eagle!" the girl said. "The greatest nerd in northern California! "He always comes when comic book fans need him most."

Dalasia spotted a dark figure on the roof deck

of the garage. Whoever it was stood just behind the waist-high ledge that ran around the edge of the roof; then the figure swept one arm out stiffly over the street below. An arm, she now saw, that seemed covered with . . . feathers?

At the same time, a deep voice boomed from the top of the parking garage.

"My brethren, I know of your distress and have heeded the call to action! Let the word go forth: Damon Wilder is unfit to don Metalman's mighty armor, and from this day forward Bald Eagle shall fight beak and talon against the casting of this impostor!"

The pirate-cat cheered.

"Nuts," said Dalasia. "Definitely nuts." She crossed her arms and waited to see what would happen next.

"All around the world am I known for my dedication to justice, my unquenchable thirst for righteousness, and my unbending opposition to unnecessary franchise reboots and bad casting," the figure bellowed. He leaned closer to the ledge and pointed in the direction of the theater. "You shall soon rue the day you brought the undefeatable, the infallible—" Dalasia noticed that the oddball was leaning pretty far over the edge now, and how stiff his movements were. Probably because of the costume, she decided.

". . . incredible, indestructible Bald Eagle down upon youAAAAHHHHHH!"

And then Bald Eagle tipped over the ledge and plummeted head-first toward the sidewalk.

The pirate-cat screamed.

Dalasia reached for her walkie-talkie.

Bald Eagle . . . flew.

For a moment, Dalasia wasn't sure what she was seeing. Instead of hitting the ground with a sickening thud, the costumed weirdo was now hovering in midair in front of the parking garage, just one story below the roof deck. About two seconds later, she realized why: the guy had a rope harness tied around his upper body; the other end was secured somewhere on the roof. The caped fool was now dangling like a fish on a hook, swinging slowly back and forth.

"A little help?" called the booming voice, sounding less than confident now.

Dalasia sighed and reached for her walkie-talkie yet again. She wasn't bored anymore. Just annoyed.

"I can't believe that worked!" DeMarco said with a giggle as he, Silas, Nick, and Tesla slinked along the trailers and trucks bordering the set.

Nick looked back nervously over his shoulder.

"We don't know for sure that it *did* yet."

"There he goes again," Silas said with a shake of the head. "Mr. Worst Cake Scenario."

"Worst-*case* scenario," Nick said. He glared at his sister, whom he resented for mentioning the nickname their mother used to call him.

If Tesla noticed her brother's dirty look, she didn't let on.

"We're in. So it worked," she said. "And hopefully Stellan and what's-his-name will get away from the garage before the cops show up. The problem is, it won't buy us much time."

"Exactly," said Nick. He pointed at the backpack DeMarco was wearing. "We need to find a place to pull that stuff out. Fast. Because if we're spotted before we can—"

"Mr. Worst-Case Scenario," Silas cut in with a chuckle.

Nick found the name incredibly annoying, but at least Silas got it right this time.

DeMarco, who was leading the group, moved around the nearest trailer—the biggest, sleekest one on the set—and dared to peek out at the P.A.s and technicians hurrying this way and that.

"Uh, maybe we ought to stay on this side of the trailers," said Nick.

Silas opened his mouth and said, "Mr.—"

"*Don't* say it," Nick said.

Silas closed his mouth.

"Stop being so jumpy, Nick," DeMarco said. He took a bold step around the trailer, gesturing for the others to do the same. "If you just relax, we'll blend in and—"

"Hey!" called a gruff voice.

The kids turned to see the burly Teamster, the man who had given them a hard time earlier. He was walking toward them holding a huge tool box.

"Keepin' outta trouble, *nephew?*" the man asked DeMarco.

"Trying to," DeMarco said, giving a strained laugh.

"Right on," the man said. As he passed, all four kids let out their breath.

But instantly they sucked it back in again.

Not thirty yards away, DeMarco's Aunt Zoe was

engaged in a heated discussion with the executive producer, Bob Ortmann.

DeMarco and the others whipped around, but there was Abby, the P.A. who'd driven them home earlier, and she was headed their way. She carried a tray filled with steaming coffee cups and had not spotted them yet, but in mere seconds she surely would.

"Guys?" Nick said.

He jerked his head at the trailer next to them—specifically, at the door, which was just a few steps away.

No one had time to say anything. Tesla quickly spread her arms and shoved the boys toward the door. A second later, they were inside.

"Whoa," Nick said.

Everyone else was speechless.

The interior of the trailer didn't look like a trailer at all. It looked like a cross between a deluxe suite in a fancy hotel and a Toys 'R' Us.

There was a basketball hoop and a pool table and a Metalman pinball machine and a long mahogany bar and a living room with plush couches and, taking up half a wall, the largest large-screen

TV any of them had ever seen. Hooked up to the TV via a tangle of black wires and cables were an Xbox 360, a Wii U, a PlayStation 4, a DVD player, a Blu-ray player, a VCR . . . and a squat, flat, boxy machine with the word BETAMAX written in white letters across the front.

In one corner were spiral stairs leading up to a second floor. (*A second floor? In a trailer?* Tesla thought.) In another corner was a hot tub with a beach ball and an inflatable shark floating in the water.

"Swanky!" Silas said.

"Yeah," said DeMarco, looking down at a Fritos bag lying on the couch, golden crumbs covering the cushions around it. "Real classy."

Tesla walked to one of the windows and peeked outside to see if they'd been spotted.

"This must be Damon Wilder's trailer," she said quietly. (The window was open, and she didn't want the sound of her voice drifting out to Aunt Zoe or anyone else.)

"If this is Damon Wilder's trailer," Nick said, "doesn't that mean Damon Wilder is probably—?"

"Hello?" called a voice from the second floor. "Is

someone down there?"

"—*here?*" Nick mouthed the word silently.

No one bothered answering Nick's question because the answer was obvious.

Damon Wilder was walking down the stairs.

"*Hide*," whispered Nick.

"Where?" asked DeMarco.

"Quick. Into the hot tub," said Silas.

Tesla didn't say anything. She just grabbed Silas by the arm and started dragging him toward the wooden bar, trusting that Nick and DeMarco would follow.

They did.

A second later, the four of them were crouched behind the bar. Which was fortunate, because exactly two seconds later they heard Damon Wilder say, "I could've sworn I heard something."

"Probably just some Teamster 'accidentally' banging a boompole against your door," said someone else. It took Tesla a moment to place the voice: it belonged to Jack Wiltrout, the writer who had been supplying Wilder with terrible dialogue.

"Yeah," Wilder said dismissively. "You're probably right."

Footsteps sounded on the stairs. Wiltrout was following Wilder down to the first floor.

"So," Wiltrout was saying, his nasal voice even clearer—and closer—than before. "You had notes?"

He made his way across the room and was standing on the other side of the bar. The kids could see his back and the curly brown hair atop his head. If he turned around . . .

"I love the new draft," Wilder said, "but it's missing something."

Jack Wiltrout stood stock-still.

"Like what?" he said.

"I want more angst."

"I've given you plenty of angst."

"Not enough. I want more. Lots more."

Tesla felt a tug on her shirt. She glanced around to find Silas staring at her, a confused look on his face.

He raised his hands, palms up, and shrugged.

What's "angst"? he was asking.

Tesla scowled at him and raised a finger to her lips.

(Angst, by the way, is a feeling of dread or nervousness.)

"And where will all this extra angst come from?" Wiltrout said.

"I've been thinking about that. What if I were blind?"

"Blind?"

"Yes. Blind. And mad about it. There's a big bunch of angst right there."

Wiltrout finally moved away from the bar.

"Damon, that would change *everything*," he said.

"Yes," said Wilder. "For the better."

A long silence ensued. They could hear one of the men sit down on the couch. That was followed by a loud rustling and series of *crunch, crunch, crunch* noises. Wiltrout had opened a bag and was snacking on something, probably pretzels or chips.

"Fine," he said at last. "I'll get started on a new draft immediately."

The crunching resumed, and next came the distinctive sound of someone quickly flipping through crisp new paper. "Here, on page fifty-one," Wilder was saying. "In the scene where I'm seeing my therapist. You need to add more—"

"Angst?" Jack said.

"Exactly! Angst! Now, you're—oh, my God, what is that smell?"

Tesla pinched her nose.

Nick and Silas hurriedly pinched theirs, too.

DeMarco hung his head in shame.

"Oooh," Wilder said. "What happened, Jack? Did you load up on too many doughnuts at the craft service table?"

"Oh, please," Wiltrout said, his voice even more nasal than before (because he was pinching his nose, too). "In the immortal words of the Bard: 'he who hath smelt it, dealt it.'"

"No way, man. I've never dealt anything that smelled like—wait, does that saying really come from Shakespeare? No, never mind. Let's continue this conversation upstairs in my office, where the air is fresher."

"Fine," Wiltrout said, sighing.

Tesla and the others could hear the spiral staircase creaking as the two men stepped onto it.

Nick, Tesla, and DeMarco slowly began to stand.

"By the way—"

Nick, Tesla, and DeMarco ducked again. (Silas hadn't moved.)

"I had a phone call from Bob Ortmann today," Wilder said. It sounded like the two men had stopped walking halfway up the staircase.

"Oh, really? And what did our executive producer have to say?"

"Only that *certain people*—"

"Meaning, studio executives."

"That certain people were unhappy with the all problems this production has been having."

"Meaning, they're worried about making money."

Wilder resumed walking up the stairs, followed by Wiltrout.

Nick, Tesla, and DeMarco stood again; Nick wiped his brow, signaling a silent "whew." DeMarco gestured for Silas to get up, but Silas seemed to be having trouble pushing himself off the floor.

Near the top of the staircase, the men's conversation continued. "So, what did you say to him?" It was Wiltrout's voice.

Yet again, Nick, Tesla, and DeMarco ducked back behind the bar.

"Oh, you know me, Jack. I told him the show must go on. No itchy-powder prank is going to stop Damon Wilder. Then I let him know that if *certain people* want this production to go more smoothly, they ought to fire Cash Ashkinos and Zoe Helms and get some A-listers in here."

The two men chuckled. Nick heard someone moving behind him. He turned his head and saw a frightening spectacle . . .

DeMarco was standing up. And his face was boiling red with anger.

Nick's jaw dropped. He tugged on his sister's shirt.

In full panic mode, Nick kept swiveling his head back and forth, looking at DeMarco, then at Tesla, then DeMarco, then Tesla . . . He could see that Jack Wiltrout was standing on the stairs with his back to the bar, but Damon Wilder was a few steps higher and within the sight line of their hiding place. With the curve of the spiral staircase, he might just see DeMarco from the corner of his eye. He had only to turn his head slightly to the right . . .

"*SIT DOWN, DEMARCO!*" Nick mouthed the words, folding his hands together in a silent plea. "*PLEASE.*"

"*SIT DOWN, DEMARCO!*" Tesla demanded silently, frowning with her angriest face and stabbing at the floor with both index fingers. "*NOW.*"

But DeMarco clearly wanted to flatten Wilder for badmouthing his aunt. His fists were clenched, and for the first time since they'd known him, Tesla and Nick saw the same terrifying expression on their friend's face that they'd seen many times on the faces of his sisters: that of someone prepared to dish out serious punishment. DeMarco took one step to move past Nick . . .

And then, in an instant, he sat down again.

In fact, DeMarco was yanked down. Silas had grabbed him around the waist and pulled him backward; DeMarco tumbled directly onto his large friend with a muffled *thunk*.

"Did you hear that?" Wiltrout said.

"What?"

"It sounded like a muffled *thunk*." The stairs creaked as Wiltrout took a step down.

"Jack!" Wilder said. "Let's focus on the work, okay? We've got lots of rewriting to do."

"Meaning," Wiltrout muttered, "*I've* got a lot of rewriting to do." He sighed his heaviest sigh yet as he followed Wilder up the spiral staircase and out of sight.

No one moved.

A minute ticked slowly by.

Then Tesla rose confidently to her feet.

Nick rose cautiously to his feet.

DeMarco rose nimbly to his feet.

Silas was lying on his back, like a turtle.

"They're gone," DeMarco whispered to Silas. "You can get up now."

"No, I can't," said Silas. "I think I'm permanently curled."

"Come on," DeMarco said.

He and Nick each took one of Silas's arms and pulled their friend upright.

Click-click-click-clack went his back.

"Thanks," Silas said.

"Thank *you* for stopping me from blowing my top," DeMarco said, keeping his voice low. He and Silas did their quick, secret handshake, the one that even Nick and Tesla didn't know about. "I kind of lost it there for a second."

"Come on, let's get out of here," said Nick.

He started toward the door, with DeMarco and Silas on his heels.

Tesla followed, too, but slowly, thinking hard. She felt like they'd been trying to do a connect-the-dots drawing that didn't have any numbers, only dots. Now there were a bunch of new dots on the page. She still had no idea where to draw the lines.

If she could just figure out where to start . . .

As she passed the couch, she noticed something lying next to the crumpled Fritos bag. A stack of white paper, bound together. The side facing up was blank.

It had to be the script that Wilder and Wiltrout had been discussing. She remembered hearing Wilder drop it during the "odor incident."

Something told Tesla that this might be the dot she was looking for.

She took a step to grab it.

"Stop!"

It was Jack's voice, hollering from upstairs.

"Stop with the instructions, Damon. Diet Coke with a wedge of lemon, lots of ice. I know, same as always." And then, a little louder: "I'll be back with it in a minute."

Footsteps on the stairs.

Silas and DeMarco quickly slipped out the door.

Nick stayed in the doorway, staring wide-eyed at his sister as he pinwheeled an arm wildly. She was halfway between the couch and the door and seemed unsure which way to go.

"*Let's go, Tez*," he said in a hiss.

Tesla spun away from the couch, and then she and Nick burst out into the sunshine together.

Silas and DeMarco had already begun casually strolling away from the trailer, hands in their pockets and innocent looks on their faces. Nick and Tesla quickly caught up.

"That was weird," Silas said as the four of them trotted away from Damon Wilder's trailer. "Real weird. Why would Metalman go blind? He's got cybernetically enhanced senses. And why would Metalman see a therapist? That doesn't sound like any superhero movie I've even seen. And why do they want so many ants?"

"Angst," Tesla corrected him. "But you're right, it was weird."

"Never mind all that," Nick said. "We gotta find somewhere private to get ready for phase two."

"Leave it to me," said DeMarco. "'I know one place where we can go. I had an idea while we were hiding."

"Was that before or after you decided you wanted to punch Damon Wilder?" Tesla said, annoyed. "You almost blew everything! Don't think we're not going to talk about that, because—"

But DeMarco seemed not to be listening. Instead,

he walked up to a P.A. passing by with a binder full of forms and files.

"Excuse me," DeMarco said. "Where's the restroom?"

"The honeywagons?" said the P.A. He was a twentysomething with tattooed arms and a beard so long and thick that it was almost as large as his head. He pointed at a large white truck nearby. "Go around that and turn left. You'll see 'em."

"Thanks!" said DeMarco.

"And with that bit of brilliance, DeMarco Davison totally redeems himself," Tesla said. The four friends started walking toward the truck.

"Honeywagons?" said Nick.

DeMarco shrugged. "That must be what movie people call the bathroom."

"I wonder," said Silas, "what they call the trucks that deliver honey."

When they reached the other side of the truck, Nick, Tesla, Silas, and DeMarco found out that a honeywagon wasn't just any bathroom. It was, to be more specific, a portable outdoor toilet. In this case, five blue plastic boxes lined up side by side.

Nick shuddered.

"I hate these things," he said.

"Me, too," said Tesla, waving away a fly.

"I almost fell into one once," said Silas.

Nick and Tesla looked away. Neither wanted Silas to continue with his story.

"Hey, don't complain—we needed privacy, and now we've got it," DeMarco said.

He shrugged off his backpack, unzipped it, and pulled out Bald Eagle's grappling hook and wrist launcher.

"You brought that? It's not part of phase two," Nick said.

"I know," said DeMarco. "But the way this day is going, who knows what phase three is going to look like."

He set aside the grappling hook and launcher and started pulling out the stuff they *really* needed.

"Doesn't anyone want to hear my port-a-potty story?" Silas said.

"Can't talk," Nick said. "Have to work on phase two."

"I've heard that story anyway," DeMarco added. "It stinks."

HORRIFYINGLY HORRIBLE
ALIEN ZOMBOID MAKEUP

THE STUFF

- Unflavored gelatin packets (these are usually found in the baking aisle of the supermarket)

- Small bowl and spoon for mixing

- Measuring spoons

- Hot water

- All-purpose flour

- Green and black washable poster paint

- Plastic spray bottle

- Baking soda

- White vinegar

- Dish soap

- A responsible adult to help with mixing the gelatin

THE SETUP

1. Pour a packet of the gelatin into a small bowl.

2. WARNING! ADULT HELPER NEEDED!! Ask an adult to heat some water on the stove. Carefully measure 2 tablespoons of warm water and add to the bowl.

3. Add a teaspoon of flour to the water and mix with a spoon until the mixture is smooth, similar to thick syrup.

4. The gel will thicken as it cools. Ask an adult to make sure the goo has cooled enough to touch. When it's warm, but not hot, it's ready for use.

THE FINAL STEPS

1. Use a spoon (or a pop stick leftover from the robo-arm project) to apply the zomboid makeup while it is still warm. Create textures, bumps, and scars. Be careful to keep the makeup away from your eyes.

2. If needed, mix up more small batches to cover as much skin as you want. If you make too much at once, the make-up might cool and solidify before you can use it.

3. For an extra-grotesque effect, use a sponge or cloth to apply washable green and black tempera paint, or face paint, to add color to your zomboid look. Experiment with other colors to create different zombie and alien hybrids. Use makeup borrowed from your mom (don't take it without asking!) to add dark circles around your eyes and fill in blank spots.

BONUS EFFECT

You can make your zomboid skin foam!

WARNING: USE FOAMING ZOMBOID MAKEUP *ONLY* ON YOUR HANDS! If you use it on your face, the vinegar will sting your eyes.

Here's how:

1. As the makeup sets, sprinkle a generous amount of baking soda onto the gel. (Do this step over a sink because the baking soda is likely to get all over the place.)

2. Add color to your makeup, if desired. Next, mix about a teaspoon of dish soap with a cup of vinegar and pour the mix into a spray bottle.

3. To activate the foaming, spray the makeup with the vinegar/soap solution and then watch the alien skin ooze and sizzle!

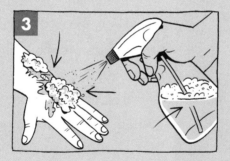

About a half hour later, four kid-sized zomboids shambled through the *Metalman* set, their faces and arms covered with the sickly green coating that was a hallmark of the alien-zombie virus.

"I can't believe that jerk Damon Wilder was trying to get my aunt fired," said the smallest of the zomboids.

"And Cash Ashkinos, too," said the biggest. "Like it's their fault that Wilder is a psycho. He's the one who has been causing all the problems!"

Two passing crew members

turned their heads to stare. But the homemade goopy makeup that Nick and Tesla had whipped up seemed to convince them that the kids belonged on the set and knew where they were going.

"Not so loud with the psycho talk," the Nick-sized zomboid said under his breath. "We can't just *look* like extras. We've got to *act* like them, too."

"And we can't blame everything on Damon Wilder, Silas," said zomboid Tesla. "Remember the itching powder? And the leaked video? Somebody's clearly trying to get him to quit, and that's the real problem."

Nick looked over at his sister.

"Do you think that's what it's all about, Tez? The reason for the video leak and the itching powder, I mean. That it's not someone just being mean to the star? It's about forcing him out of the movie?"

"I'm not sure yet," Tesla said. "Let's hypothesize. Why would someone want to get Damon Wilder kicked out?"

"Because he's a terrible actor?" Nick suggested.

"And difficult to work with?" added Tesla.

"And a complete and utter kook?" Silas threw in. "What? I want to hippopotamus, too."

"Okay. All true," DeMarco said. "But who is responsible?"

They all looked at one another.

Each one was stumped.

"Hey, check it out," DeMarco said.

He had noticed a sign taped to the side of a motor home parked to his left. The sign—really just a sheet of paper fluttering in the breeze that was blowing in off the ocean a mile away—displayed a single word printed in large, blocky letters.

MAKEUP

The door to the motor home was open. Through the doorway, the kids could see a purple-haired woman sitting in one of several large chairs lined up in front of a row of mirrors. It was Barbara, the makeup artist who'd stepped up to put face powder on Damon Wilder just before his itch-attack in the Metalman suit. She was leafing through a magazine called the *Hollywood Reporter* while sipping from a bottle of Snapple through a pink crazy straw.

The kids ambled casually past the door and then doubled back, keeping out of sight behind a few garbage cans.

"What now?" Silas said.

"Now we wait for an opportunity," said Tesla. "Then we go in and look for itching powder, like we did in the special effects trailer."

"Yeah. Because *that* worked out so well," said DeMarco sarcastically.

"We don't even know why this makeup lady would be mad at Damon Wilder," Silas pointed out. "What's her motive?"

"You said yourself: Wilder's a kook," Tesla shot back. "Who knows what kind of crazy thing he might have blown up at her about?"

Silas shook his head, looking skeptical.

"Seems pretty thin. You could say that about everybody on this movie set."

Tesla tried not to show how much his comment stung. Having your logic criticized by Silas . . . and, even worse, he's *right*? Ouch. Nick seemed to sense how his sister felt. "Don't feel bad, Tez," he said. "Silas makes a good point, which obviously means you're having a positive effect on him. He's becoming a critical thinker!"

"It's true," Silas answered. "Before I met you

guys, I hardly ever had to figure out who committed a crime. Now I'm doing it, like, every other week."

"Aaaaanyway," Nick said, "we didn't find itching powder in Matt Gore's trailer, and getting trapped in Damon Wilder's trailer didn't get us any useful info—" He noticed his sister was wearing her "I'm concentrating" frown. "Did it?" he asked her.

"I'm not sure yet."

"So, it seems worth a try to investigate the make-up lady, unless somebody has a better idea."

"I wasn't thinking past sneaking back onto the set," DeMarco admitted. "After that, I just figured . . . I don't know. Stuff would happen."

"Well, here we are," said Nick. "So, let's see about the stuff, okay?"

Silas and DeMarco nodded mutely.

Tesla suddenly snapped her fingers. "You know what else bothers me about what Damon Wilder and Jack Whatever-His-Name-Is were talking about? Besides all the angst, I mean. Wilder said that the second act was slow or sluggish or something like that. Like it was a play, not the Metalman screenplay."

Nick looked intrigued for a moment, but by the time Tesla was done talking he was shaking his head.

"Screenplays are broken into acts, too," he said. "They just don't make it obvious, like they do with plays, where there's intermissions and stuff."

"Really?"

"Yeah, he's totally right," Silas said. "All movies have three acts. In the first, you show who the good guys are and who the bad guys are. In the second, the good guys and the bad guys fight, and the good guys lose. In the third, everything starts exploding, and the good guys win."

"And that's every movie?" Tesla said skeptically.

"Well, sometimes stuff explodes in the first and second acts, too," Silas conceded. "But, yeah—that's pretty much every movie."

"Not *The Wizard of Oz*," said Nick.

"Not *E.T.*," said Tesla.

"Not *The Avengers*," said DeMarco. "Oh, wait. That is totally *The Avengers*."

Silas nodded smugly. "And *The Wizard of Oz* and *E.T.*, too. You just have to look for the—"

"ZOMBOIDS!"

All four kids jumped. The bellowing voice belonged to a muscular woman wearing a white tank top and jeans, her head topped by a baseball cap featuring the logo of a mountain surrounded by stars. In one hand, she held a clipboard. In the other hand was a walkie-talkie.

She was glaring at the four kids with the sort of expression a person usually reserves for a bug found in your food. "You guys are unbelievable," she said, shaking her head. "Come with me."

"Well, stuff is happening," said DeMarco, sighing unhappily as the woman led them away. "So, I guess the plan *kind* of worked . . . ."

The production assistant marched Nick, Tesla, DeMarco, and Silas past the trailers and trucks and lighting rigs and food tables that the kids had come to know so well that day. Every dozen paces or so, she checked over her shoulder to make sure her prisoners were still in tow.

They were. It was no use making a break for it. Each of them, in his or her own way, was thinking the same thing.

"*Well, it's all over,*" Tesla was thinking.

"*We've been caught, and the culprit hasn't,*" Nick was thinking.

"*My aunt's going to be fired, and my mom's going to kill me,*" DeMarco was thinking.

"*I wonder if Stardust the Super-Wizard and Fantomah, Mystery Woman of the Jungle, are married,*" Silas was thinking. "*Also, now we'll never get a chance to save Cash Ashkinos and Aunt Zoe from certain doom!*"

The only question was whether the P.A. was about to hand them over to the local police (a 15 percent probability, in Nick's estimation), simply kick them off the set (25 percent), or let Aunt Zoe yell at them for a while and *then* kick them off the set (59 percent). Being a good, conservative statistician, Nick factored in a 1 percent margin of error.

When the P.A. did none of those things—instead leading them to the old theater the movie crew had taken over—Nick was dumbfounded. She shooed them into the lobby, where two dozen other "zomboids," all wearing makeup similar to that on the four friends, were waiting around. "This is our last shot for today, and you almost missed it. Next time, don't just stand around waiting when Makeup's through with you. Get to your marks," the woman said. Then she spun on her heel and walked briskly away.

"She just . . . ," Nick said, too stunned to put their good luck into words.

Tesla finished his sentence for him.

"—assumed we were zomboid extras in the wrong place! I should have realized what was happening. After all, we made this makeup so that we'd look like the other zomboids."

"Stuff is happening!" Silas said.

He turned to DeMarco and gave him a high-five.

"We caught a break, all right. But now we're stuck here," said Tesla.

A hand reached out and tapped her on the shoulder.

It was a green hand, with a large veiny patch of dangling skin.

Tesla turned and found herself staring into the bright yellow eyes of a fortyish man with an olive-tinted face and grotesquely wrinkled skin. He was dressed as a movie theater employee, in a white shirt and a black vest and a little bow tie and a name tag that said FRANK.

"Hi, I'm Paul!" the zomboid said cheerfully. "You guys are new, huh?"

"Uh, yeah," said Tesla.

"Well, you probably better stay in the back when they roll again." They've already got lots of footage of the first zomboids running out of the theater. And if you four are suddenly out in front in the next shot—"

"I get it," said DeMarco. "It won't match the other shots."

"Continuity error!" said Silas.

The zomboid nodded.

"Exactly."

He looked the kids up and down, his gaze lingering a little longer than Nick liked on a sweaty-shiny spot on Silas's forehead, where the makeup didn't quite reach his scalp.

"You're not professionals, are you?" Paul said.

Silas smirked. "He's the line producer's nephew," he said, pointing at DeMarco.

"Well," Paul said, "if you need any help from a *professional*, just let me know. I've been a background artist in twenty-six feature films and seventy-nine episodics."

"Background artist?" said Silas.

"Episodics?" said DeMarco.

Paul focused his mustard-yellow eyes on DeMarco.

"Episodic television series," he said. "I've been

a dead body on *Crime Lab: San Francisco* eight times alone. The casting directors say I'm the best stiff in the Bay Area."

"Background artist?" Silas said again.

Paul's jaw clenched as he shifted his head to look at Silas.

"A film and television performer who specializes in peripheral nonspeaking roles," he explained.

"Oh," said Silas. "You mean an extra."

Several of the other zomboids nearby turned to frown at Silas. One of them even growled, though she may have been practicing her undead speech patterns.

"No," Paul said icily. "A background artist. And contrary to what *some people* believe, it's not something any untrained fourth-grader can do at the drop of a hat. It requires skill, commitment, and creativity. Now, if you'll excuse me, I need to get back into character."

Paul turned and shuffled away, moaning.

"Stop calling attention to yourself," Nick said to Silas.

"And annoying people," DeMarco added.

"But those just happen to be two of my best-developed skills," Silas replied with great dignity.

"We should probably move away from the doors, like that Paul guy suggested," Nick said. "There'll be less chance that Aunt Zoe or Matt Gore or somebody walking by will recognize us."

"But what's the point of staying at all?" DeMarco said. "It's not like we're going to solve the mystery by hanging around here. Right, Tez?"

Tesla said nothing.

"Tez?" Nick said, leaning close to look into his sister's eyes.

They were glassy, vacant.

"She must be getting into character, too," Silas said. "I think I'll try it."

He began to drool.

"I'm not getting into character," Tesla finally said. "I'm *listening*."

"Listening?" Silas said. "To what?"

Nick and DeMarco shushed him. Then all three boys started listening, too.

There was only one thing to hear. Not far away, two background artists were trading gossip.

" . . . friend worked with Damon on *The Witches of Greenwich Village*," said one, a woman with an English accent. "And she said the same thing as you: he was very professional, very skilled. Not a nut job, like he is now."

"So what went wrong?" snorted a man with a deep, gravelly voice.

"The money's gone to his head, I expect. I heard one of the P.A.s say he got $3 million for this movie."

"I heard the assistant director say $5 million, pay or play."

"Ooooh," the woman cooed. "Pay or play for his first lead role in a feature? He must have a good agent."

"Silas," Tesla said quietly. "Go over to those zomboids and ask what 'pay or play' means."

"Why me?" Silas said.

"Because a minute ago you said that you don't mind calling attention to yourself and annoying people."

"Oh. Yeah. Right. Okay."

Silas turned and took a step toward the two zomboids, who were sitting together on the floor, their backs against the wall.

"Excuse me. What's 'pay or play'? Is that, like, a sports thing?"

"If you have a pay-or-play contract," the man lectured gruffly, "it means that you get paid no matter what."

Silas furrowed his brow.

"Don't actors always get paid no matter what?"

The woman shook her head.

"Not if the studio puts the project in turnaround. Meaning, it decides not to make the movie," the man explained.

"Or can't get the film into production before your contract expires," the woman said. "Or they decide to dump you for a bigger star at the last minute."

"Wow," Silas said. "So you could get replaced and not get paid even if you've been working on the movie from the beginning? That stinks. Maybe I should stick to being a director instead of a director-actor-producer-cameraman."

"All right, Silas," Tesla whispered. "That's enough."

"Let me ask you guys something," Silas continued, pointedly ignoring Tesla and turning back to the others. "When you're playing a zomboid, is it better to stick your arms out like this"—he held both arms straight out in front, as if he were Frankenstein—"or let them hang at your sides like this?" Silas dropped his arms and let them dangle limply while he shuffled around, zombie-like.

"Silas, you can stop now," Tesla hissed.

But instead of stopping, Silas walked over to the zomboids and sat down beside them. "What do you think?"

Immediately, his two new friends began debating the merits of zomboid arm placement.

"Great," DeMarco said with a groan. "We're trying to save my aunt's career, and Silas decides to sit around and swap acting tips."

"Let him do his thing," Nick said. "We've got planning to do."

"We do?" said DeMarco.

Nick nodded and then looked at his sister.

"I think we just solved the mystery by hanging around with a bunch of background artists," she said. "Now, it's time to go get the proof."

"Looks like we've moved on to phase three!" DeMarco said.

SUPERHEROIC GRAPPLING HOOK AND WRIST LAUNCHER

THE STUFF

- 1 plastic water or soda bottle (one that's smooth, about as wide around as your arm, and made of thick hard-to-crush plastic)

- 1 ballpoint pen

- 1 marker cap (The cap must be wider than the pen. Note: You won't be able to use the cap on the marker anymore!)

- 1 clothespin

- 3 paper clips

- 1 sturdy rubber band

- 1 spool of button thread

- 1 pushpin

- 1 old tube sock

- Hot-glue gun

- Sandpaper

- Scissors

- Pliers

- Safety goggles

- For adults only: power drill

1. Cut out a 7-inch (18 cm) long shape from the plastic bottle, as shown. This will be the base of the launcher.

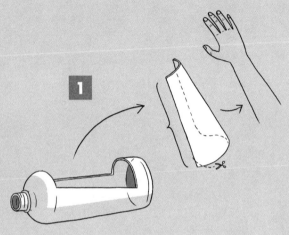

2. Use the sandpaper to smooth out any pointy corners so that they don't poke you.

3. Use the pliers to remove the front end and ink cartridge from the pen. Remove the back cap as well (cut it off, if necessary).

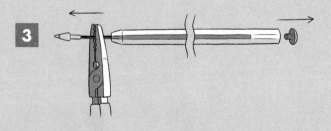

4. Unbend the paper clips as shown. Push the smaller ends into the pen tube, spacing the clips equally to form a grappling hook. Use hot glue to secure the paper clips in place in the tube.

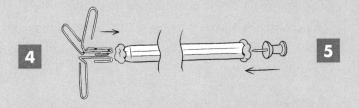

5. Use hot glue to attach the pushpin to the other end of the pen, as shown. If the pushpin is wider than the pen, rub sandpaper on the edges until the pen and the pushpin are the same width.

6. Push or cut out the end of the marker cap, or ask a grown-up to carefully cut or drill it, so that you end up with an empty tube. (The inside of the cap must be wider than the pen.)

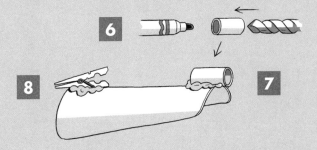

7. Use hot glue to attach the marker cap to the front of the launcher base so that about a third of the cap extends over the front edge of the launcher base.

8. Insert your grappling hook into the marker cap. Position the clothespin on the base, where it will grip the end of the pushpin while the grappling hook is pushed as far back through the marker cap as it can go. Mark that spot and glue the clothespin there.

9. Cut the toe end off the sock, leaving a sleeve about as long as the launcher base.

10. Use hot glue to secure the sock to the underside of the launcher base so that you can wear the launcher comfortably on your forearm.

11. Cut off about 15 feet (4.5 m) of the button thread and tie one end securely to the pushpin. Feed the other end through the marker cap and knot it securely.

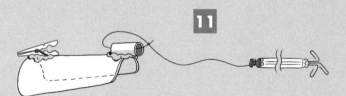

THE FINAL STEPS

1. Wrap the rubber band around the front of the cap, as shown.

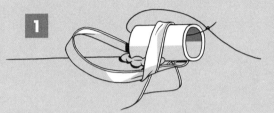

2. Wind the thread around the front of the cap, in front of the rubber band, leaving enough slack to insert the pen into the launcher.

3. Push the pen into the marker cap and stretch the rubber band with the pin to create tension. Then clip the pushpin and rubber band in place with the clothespin.

4. Your grappling hook is now ready! To launch it, simply point at a target and push down on the back of the clothespin to release the grappler. Remember to ALWAYS

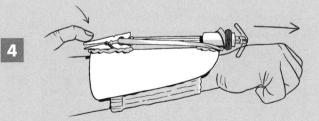

wear safety goggles (you have to watch out for ricochets!) and NEVER point the grappling hook at anyone.

5. If needed, experiment with different sizes of rubber bands, or different placements of the clothespin, to give your grappler the force it needs for a long flight.

Once they had worked out the details of phase three, Nick and Tesla went to retrieve Silas from his new friends, who were describing what it was like to play terrified onlookers in a monster-movie crowd scene.

"There's lots of pointing and screaming and running," said the zomboid woman. "It's fun."

"I always lose my voice by the end of the first day, but that's okay," said the zomboid man. "The sound editors usually dub in other people's screams anyway."

Nick and Tesla each grabbed

one of Silas's arms and hauled him to his feet.

"Sorry, we've gotta go," said Nick.

"Aww, but I'm learning so much about making movies!"

"Later, Silas," Tesla said. "We've got something more important to learn right now."

As Nick and Tesla dragged Silas away, they bumped into Paul, the professional "background artist" they'd met earlier.

"Where do you think you're going?" he demanded.

"Our friend seems to be having a bad reaction to the makeup," Nick said.

He nodded at DeMarco, who was standing by the doors. The zomboid makeup on his hands and arms seemed to be sizzling and smoking.

"I'm melting," DeMarco groaned. "Mellllllting."

Even through all the makeup Paul was wearing, it was plain that the blood had drained from his face.

"Oh, geez," he said hoarsely. "The set medic should be out by Video Village. You'd better hurry."

"Thanks!" Nick said.

"And tell the people in Makeup to come check on the rest of us!" Paul called out.

Nick gave him a thumbs-up. "Will do."

"Oh, what a world, what a world," DeMarco whimpered as he staggered onto the sidewalk.

"Oh, all right, all right," Tesla said. "We've seen enough overacting for one day."

"We have to remember to use that effect in *Bald Eagle: The Legend Takes Flight*," said Silas. "Will it take long for DeMarco's burns to heal?"

"He's not on fire," said Nick. "Adding vinegar to the zomboid makeup makes it sizzle like that."

"Even better," Silas said.

By now, the kids had been through the set enough times to know the best route. Dart around the first trailer, hop over the cables leading from the big humming generator, and you could move along the edge and avoid most of the crew. And that's just what they did.

In less than a minute, they'd reached their destination: the honeywagons, where they had stashed DeMarco's backpack, behind the cleanest port-a-potty. They pulled out the bag and opened it, and then Nick and Tesla filled Silas in on the scheme while DeMarco scrubbed the bubbling makeup off his arms.

"Better hope the windows in Damon Wilder's trailer are still open," Silas said after he'd heard the first part of the plan. "And that the evidence is still there. And that Wilder isn't just sitting inside next to it. Otherwise, it's game over."

Nick placed a hand on Silas's broad shoulder.

"I'm impressed," Nick said. "You really are getting the hang of pointing out the worst-case scenario."

"I've been learning from the master," said Silas.

Tesla shifted a stony gaze from Nick to Silas and back to Nick again, trying to decide which one was more annoying.

Silas set off on his mission.

DeMarco set off on his mission.

Nick and Tesla set off on their mission: Damon Wilder's trailer.

"Let's do this thing," said Nick, his voice cracking on "thing."

"Hey, that's my line," said Tesla.

"I know. You're always saying stuff like that. I just wanted to try it once."

"How does it feel?"

Nick thought it over. "Kinda weird. You say it."

"*Let's do this thing,*" Tesla said firmly.

Nick nodded. "Yeah, that's more like it."

When they reached the trailer, Nick and Tesla took up position in the narrow gap between the structure and the truck parked beside it. Crew members moved by in their usual hurry; none were paying attention to the two mini zomboid extras just standing around.

"Ready?" said Tesla.

"Ready," said Nick. "It's time to get to work." His voice cracked on "work."

"Dang it," he said, sighing.

Shielded (a bit) by a newspaper that Tesla was pretending to read (the *San Francisco Chronicle*, whose headline read "Artisanal Toast Raises Dough"), Nick and his sister peered toward the trailer's windows.

"Whew," Nick said. "They're still open."

The pair checked to see that the coast was clear, and then they stepped closer to the windows. Tesla held up the newspaper and Nick stood behind her.

"Well?" she said.

"Well—" Nick started to speak, but a loud and familiar voice interrupted him.

"Well, well, well!"

Tesla lowered the newspaper to see the beefy, flannel-shirted Teamster who'd been giving them a rough time all day. He was standing there staring at her and Nick, his big hands set on his hips.

"Look at you two zomboids," he said. "Know a producer's nephew, and suddenly you're in the movies."

"Uh, I guess," said Nick.

"That's Hollywood for ya," said Tesla.

They both laughed nervously.

"Well, what are you doing here? You lost?" the Teamster asked. He jerked his thumb to the right. "They're shooting down that way."

"Oh, we're not lost," said Nick. "We're . . . uh . . ."

"Waiting," said Tesla.

The Teamster squinted at them. "Waiting for what?"

"Well . . . ," Tesla said.

But before she could get something, *anything* else to come out of her mouth, the expression on the

Teamster's face changed from suspicious and curious to sly and amused.

He looked from Nick and Tesla to the open window of Wilder's trailer and back again.

He knows, Tesla thought. *Oh, no, he knows!*

"You know what?" he said. "Never mind." And then he turned and started to leave. After a few steps, he paused to glance back.

"Good luck. I'll be keeping an eye on YouTube."

He gave the kids a big wink and then walked away.

"Uhh . . . what just happened?" Nick said.

"He thinks we're trying to spy on Wilder!" Tesla said. "Maybe to get more embarrassing video to leak online."

"Boy, people sure do hate that guy."

"Can you blame them?"

"Not really," Nick said. "Anyway, it's go time." Nick grinned. His voice didn't crack.

Tesla opened her newspaper again, and Nick stepped behind her. Its Pulitzer Prize–winning reportage wouldn't provide them much cover, but it was better than nothing.

Tesla waited for the soft *sproinggg* of Nick shooting the grappling hook through the open window and into the trailer.

"Tez!"

"Did you get it?" She didn't want to turn around; it was important to keep watching for anyone coming to interrupt them.

"Tez!"

"Nick, if you missed, just aim better."

"Tez!"

"What? What's the problem? What happened to 'It's go time'?"

"Tez, it's not here! Wilder's script isn't here!"

Behind Damon Wilder's trailer stood two giant plastic trash bins, the kind with built-in wheels and an attached lid. Besides being strong enough to hold refuse of all sorts, the bins made a perfect cover for two zomboid kids to hide behind while discussing their next step.

"Without that script, we've got nothing," Nick was saying. "It's the key to the whole thing! Even with it, we'll need to do a lot of explaining . . ."

"Maybe it's somewhere else in the trailer," Tesla said. "If we sneak in—"

"Tez, I'm not even sure it was right to try to steal the script through the window, even if Damon Wilder is up to no good. But sneaking in there again and going through his stuff . . . no way. Besides, if we got caught, nobody would listen to anything we had to say. We might even get thrown in jail for burglary and—"

"Easy, Nick, easy," Tesla said, putting her hands on his shoulders. "Nobody's going to jail. Take a breath."

"This whole thing is stupid," he said. "A big waste of time. We should be trying to find Mom and Dad. I should be back at the house doing research online. Except *you* had to fritz up the computer."

"Nick, we talked about that."

"I know, I know. All this is practice. I get it. But if you ask me, it's a failed experiment. Negative results. It's time to bail. Take our data and go home."

"Nick, I'm not ready."

"Come on, Tez, you—" But the look on his sister's face made him stop short. He'd hardly ever seen her look this way.

She looked scared.

"Tez?"

She lowered her eyes. "Nick, listen. I didn't just mean that I was afraid of failure. It's also that I'm *afraid*, plain and simple. Not only that Mom and Dad are mixed up in something too big for us to help with. What if they're involved in something awful and scary and really dangerous? When I think about that, I—I have trouble doing anything." When she looked up, her face was calm again, but Nick could see the anxiety in her eyes. "So, I think I end up getting involved in stuff like this because I don't want to think about what might be happening with them."

Now it was Nick's turn to put his hand on Tesla's shoulder. "Tez," he said, "I'm scared about it, too. But I'm always worrying about things, so I'm used to it. Take it from me—it's possible to be worried about something and still try to do something about it."

Her eyes narrowed as she tried to process what her brother had said. "Really?"

"Really. So, don't worry."

At that, they both laughed. "Okay," Tesla said. "Whoo. Well, let's get away from these trash bins and—" But before she could finish her sentence, the trash bins suddenly started moving away. Nick and Tesla jumped to their feet and spotted a tall man, dressed in coveralls and listening to an iPod, wheeling them away.

Their hiding place was exposed! No one seemed to notice, though. Everyone around was rushing to and fro to and didn't care that two zomboid "background artists" had wandered off the set. It was getting late in the day, and they all had long lists of tasks that still needed to be completed.

"Tez!" Nick said, "look!"

The trash guy, dragging the bins behind him, hadn't noticed that one of the lids had flopped open. He was too busy nodding his head to the rhythms of whatever he was listening to.

"Pa pa mmm mow mow, pa pa mmm mow mow mow . . . ," he half sung, half hummed.

"Come on!" said Nick, dashing toward the man, who was by then several yards away.

"What?" Tesla said as she jogged alongside him. "Where are we going?"

"Look!" Nick repeated, pointing to the trash bins. And then Tesla saw it, on top of the trash in the open bin: a white piece of paper. No, an entire stack of white papers, stapled together. The script!

The trash guy was moving quickly, but the twins got close enough for Tesla to make out the title typed on the cover page: *Reflections of Remembrance: A Play in Three Acts* by Jack Wiltrout.

"Get it!" Tesla said.

"Got it!" Nick replied. And then he reached out . . .

But he didn't get it. Suddenly, a barrier appeared between the twins and the trash bins. The roadblock was made of clothing—pants and shirts mostly, a few sweater vests, all hanging from a wheeled rack that a bored-looking P.A. was pushing across their path. Nick and Tesla skidded to a stop just in time to avoid colliding with the wall of wardrobe. Then, just when *that* obstruction rolled past them, another roadblock slid in from the *other* direction. This time, it was an actual wall; or, rather, a plywood and canvas frame painted to look like a wall. Despite its materials, it was still solid enough to block Nick and Tesla's way.

"Oh, *come on*," Nick said, rolling his eyes.

"We'll go around," Tesla said, but the two guys carrying the wall had already moved out of the twins' way, and it didn't seem like any other obstructions were heading in their direction. Yet Nick and Tesla still didn't move because now they had *another* problem.

The trash bins were nowhere to be seen!

"No!" Nick shouted. "We were so close."

"I thought you said this was a waste of time," Tesla said, scanning the area for any sign of the trash man and his cargo.

"Well, DeMarco's our friend," Nick said. He was searching the crowd, too. There were trailers and trucks and small tents all over the place. "And his aunt needs our help. We can't just bail on them. I guess I didn't really want to quit; I was just getting frustrated is all."

"There!" Tesla blurted out suddenly. She pointed at a panel van parked at the far end of the wide lane they'd been following. Nick looked over just in time to see a big blue trash receptacle disappearing behind it.

Off they ran.

Dalasia the security guard was having a strange week. She usually spent her workday watching the entrance to a warehouse, parking lot, office park, or some other place that people rarely had any interest in sneaking into. But since she'd been assigned to monitor the entrance to the *Metalman* movie set, she'd met the famous film director Cash Ashkinos (nice, but busy); got a close-up look at the movie star Damon Wilder (ignored her as he walked by); listened to a P.A. describe her movie script about a postapocalyptic Goldilocks (the ending needed work); and made friends with a movie producer (a nice lady who got her the star's autograph and promised to send her tickets when the movie came out). She'd also chased away autograph seekers and other lookie-loos, put up with annoying chants from people dressed in weird costumes (a pirate cat? What *was* that?), and almost called the fire department to rescue what turned out to be a bird costume stuffed with newspapers.

Things had finally calmed down, and Dalasia's shift would be over in another hour. Even better, she'd found one last Sudoku puzzle in her book, which she'd overlooked. With luck, things would stay quiet and she could work on the brain teaser until quitting time. She settled back in her folding chair and erased the number she'd just written in her puzzle book.

"Excuse me."

Dalasia jumped from her chair. She didn't see anybody across the street or up or down the sidewalk, either.

"Excuse me, ma'am," the voice said again. Dalasia turned around, and that's when she saw Tesla Holt, standing behind the temporary fence. Tesla was still wearing her alien zombie makeup, so Dalasia had only the slightest feeling that she'd seen this kid before.

"I thought they finished filming the zombie scene," Dalasia said, resting one hand on her walkie-talkie and holding her Sudoku book in the other.

"It's zom*boid*," Tesla said. "Yeah, they finished. I'm just waiting around for my—my uncle to come and pick me up."

"Okay," Dalasia said. "Well, they'll probably be closing everything down for the day pretty soon, so you should get back to Makeup and have them take that goop off your face." Dalasia smiled. *I sound like I work in Hollywood*, she thought.

"I will," Tesla said. "But I noticed that you have a puzzle book, and I was wondering . . ." She walked up to the sawhorses, standing to the side so that Dalasia had to turn to face her. "Can you show me how to do Sudoku? I've been wanting to learn, but I don't really get it."

"Oh," Dalasia said, "sure! Sudoku is great! Are you good with puzzles?"

"Are you kidding?" Tesla said with a shrug. "I mean, kinda." As Dalasia approached, opening her puzzle book, Tesla glanced past the security guard's shoulder. Less than a stone's throw away was a huge Dumpster, piled with trash. And on top of the pile, gleaming in the late afternoon sun like a bright white diamond, was the script that she and Nick had been chasing all over the place. It had been a wild pursuit, taking them through the maze of trailers and trucks; dangerously close to Video Village (where Aunt Zoe and Cash Ashkinos were having an argument and an army of P.A.s were skittering everywhere, each one holding a tray of lattes); and, finally, here, on the outskirts of the set. For a moment, all had seemed lost as the trash guy dumped everything into the rusted Dumpster, but miraculously the script ended up on top of the heap.

"Wow, even the garbage doesn't want it," Nick had whispered.

But then they noticed that the security guard was stationed just a few paces away. The Dumpster was huge, and the script was too high for either Nick or Tesla to reach it from ground level. Climbing onto the Dumpster would surely make noise—maybe even cause a trash avalanche—that would attract the guard's notice. So they made a plan, flipped a coin, and now Tesla had to keep Dalasia occupied while Nick used the Bald Eagle grappler to pull down the script.

"So, you just put in any numbers you want?" Tesla said.

"Oh, no," Dalasia said. "It's much more complicated than that. Here, let me show you this last one I'm working on . . ." In reality, Tesla had mastered Sudoku a year ago and was already bored with it. In fact, she'd moved on to UltraMegaSudoku, which was played on a cube instead of a square and involved fractions. She was having trouble coming up with questions to ask the guard.

Nick, meanwhile, had crept as close to the Dumpster as he dared. Any nearer, and he wouldn't be at the right angle to hit the script with the grappling hook. Unfortunately, because of the script's location, Nick had to stand out in the open, in full view of the security guard if she turned around.

Tesla was asking Dalasia whether Sudoku had anything to do with tofu when she saw Nick raise the grappler . . . aim . . . fire . . .

On its release the grappling hook went low, careening off the side of the Dumpster.

Dalasia's head snapped up. "What was that?"

"Huh?" Tesla resisted the urge to flash an angry look in Nick's direction. *Reload*, she was thinking, *and fire again.*

"I thought I heard a weird noise," Dalasia said, scanning the street behind Tesla. "Like . . . something careening off of something."

Do not turn around, Tesla was saying in her head. She saw Nick fire again; this time, the grappling hook arced high, landing somewhere in the piled-up trash. Nick started pulling it in ever so gingerly.

Hurry up, Tesla thought. But aloud she said,

"Look!" She pointed at the Sudoku page. "Didn't you make a mistake there?"

"Huh?" Dalasia inspected the puzzle. "Well I'll be . . . you're right. I used a three twice in that row. Must have been when those weird boys dangled that bird-dummy off the parking garage."

Tesla's head snapped up. "Did they get caught?" she said. "I mean, whoever they were."

"The police took them to the station," Dalasia said, "just to give them a little scare and a talking-to. They didn't do any harm, really." She was tapping at the puzzle with a pencil she'd produced from her pocket. "Now, if this isn't a three, then . . ."

"Gahhh!" Tesla gasped suddenly. Nick had reeled in the grappling hook, but all he'd accomplished was to knock an empty plastic soda bottle off the trash pile. He gave Tesla a nervous wave.

"What?" Dalasia said, looking up.

"Oh," Tesla said quickly. "Numbers! So frustrating! Am I right?"

Nick was reloading the grappling hook, but it looked like the line was tangled.

"Well, if puzzles were easy, then they wouldn't be any fun to solve, would they?" Dalasia turned her attention back to the Sudoku page, erasing some of the numbered squares.

"You got that right," Tesla said. She had already solved the puzzle in her head, and it was taking all of her self-control not to grab the pencil from Dalasia's hand and fill in the missing numbers.

Nick was taking aim again.

Suddenly, a loud burst of static crackled over the airwaves. "HEWITT!"

Dalasia pulled the walkie-talkie from her belt. "Hewitt here."

"Morely's on the way to relieve you."

"Already? She's a half hour early."

"Yeah, I know. I need you to walk the perimeter one more time before you leave. There's been all kinds of nutty stuff going on today. Somebody says they saw a couple of zombies peeping into Wilder's trailer."

"They're called zom*boids*," Dalasia said, correcting him.

"Whatever. Just do a patrol before you clock out."

"Will do, chief." She started to put the radio back in its holster, but another burst of static signaled that the communication was not yet done.

"Don't call me chief!"

"Sorry."

"My title is supreme squad commander."

"Right, 10-4, sir. Over and out." Dalasia holstered the radio and then shrugged. "That's just a made-up title he invented," she said. She glanced at the puzzle book for a moment, then looked back at Tesla. "Wait a minute . . . zomboids?"

Tesla, meanwhile, was watching Nick. From the corner of her eye she could see that he was crouched on the ground, but she didn't dare turn her head to get a clear view of what was going on. Was the grappler broken?

"You wouldn't know anything about peeping zomboids, would you?" Dalasia said. "What did you say your name was?"

"Who, me?"

Behind her, Nick stood up. Tesla risked turning her head just a little bit . . . and that's when she saw what Nick was doing: he was waving the script!

"Yeah, you."

"I, uh . . . hey! Look." Tesla took the pencil that Dalasia had left resting in the puzzle book and began filling in numbers. "I think I figured it out."

"Now, wait a minute . . . ." Dalasia reached for the pencil but then stopped. "Say, that's right . . . and there . . . yeah! You did it!"

"I guess you're a good teacher," Tesla said. Dalasia had taken back the book and was looking over each of the numbers.

"I've been working on this for an hour . . ."

"Well, you were probably depending too much on trial and error instead of using intersection removal and chaining strategies," Tesla said.

"Wha—?"

Tesla began walking away. "Anyway, I'm going to go get this makeup off my face. Thanks for teaching me Sudoku!"

Dalasia watched the zomboid girl stride confidently back toward the set. She reached for her walkie-talkie, but then changed her mind. "Eh," she muttered. "I'm ready to call it quits for the day. Let the supreme squad commander deal with it."

Nick and Tesla paused just long enough to wash off their green makeup. (Not only did they not need it anymore, but also it was starting to itch.) Then they hurried off to see if Silas was waiting for them at the rendezvous: a dark alley that was growing ever darker as the sun sank lower in the sky.

Silas *was* there. And it was obvious that he'd successfully completed his mission, too. In his arms was a pile of scratched silver and blue metal—the armor they'd helped rip off Damon Wilder's squirming body earlier that day.

"How'd you get it?" Tesla said.

"Piece of cake. It was in a Dumpster behind Matt's trailer."

Nick squinted at Silas's face. His skin didn't look green; Silas had taken the time to wipe off his make-up, too. But something new had taken the makeup's place. A moist black smear ran across Silas's fore-head, and the curly hair above was dusted with small black specks.

"I think I also found all of Matt's old coffee grounds," Silas said. "Dumpster diving has its dangers, you know."

"Tell me about it," Nick said.

A nearby door creaked open.

"Good. You're here," DeMarco said. "Come on." The corridor beyond him was even darker than the alley, but the friends didn't hesitate. They darted inside.

DeMarco closed the door, sealing them into near-total blackness.

"This way," he said.

DeMarco led them toward a vertical stripe of light at the other end of the long, narrow hallway.

It was another door, propped open a few inches

by an ancient soda cup tipped on its side. When Nick and Tesla reached the opening, they peeked through the crack.

They were inside the Veranda Theater. On the other side of the door were rows and rows of dingy upholstered chairs and, behind them, a tall black wall pierced with a single window in the center. Through the window, the kids could see a bearded projectionist fiddling with bulky machinery, getting ready to show that day's *Metalman* footage.

All told, fewer than twenty people were in the audience. Aunt Zoe and Cash Ashkinos were sitting together in the front row. Bob Ortmann was seated one row behind them. About a half dozen other people were sprinkled throughout the seats; they saw Matt Gore and Barbara the makeup lady, as well as various members of the camera crew. Several P.A.s were standing in the side aisles, leaning against the walls and holding notebooks, tablet computers, and trays filled with even more lattes.

And walking in and making their way down one of the aisles were Damon Wilder and Jack Wiltrout.

"How are we going to make them listen to us?" DeMarco asked.

"We'll just have to pretend like we're in a movie," said Silas. "We need to be loud, hyper, and dumb."

Wilder was holding a chunk of bagel in one hand, and as he walked toward the front of the theater, he stuffed it into his mouth.

"Well, I'm here," he announced as he chewed. "Bob, is there something you want to tell me?"

"Oh. Well. Yes. Yes, there is, buddy," Bob Ortmann said. He stole an apprehensive glance at Aunt Zoe and Cash Ashkinos in the row ahead of him and then started to rise from his seat. "There's something I need to announce to everyone. We're going to have some personnel changes . . ."

"This is it!" DeMarco said. "He's gonna fire Aunt Zoe!"

"And Cash!" said Silas.

"They're not fired yet," said Nick. "Let's go, Tez!"

He was very pleased with how his voice sounded. There was almost no warble at all.

Nick burst through the doorway, with Tesla at his side and Silas and DeMarco at his heels.

"Stop!" Nick shouted. His voice cracked so much that it sounded more like "Steeoop!"

"Darn it!" he said.

"What the—?" said Bob Ortmann.

"Who the—?" said Barbara the makeup lady.

"How the—?" said Aunt Zoe.

Only Matt Gore managed to blurt out a complete sentence.

"What are you kids doing here?" he said, staring in wide-eyed wonderment at them.

"Exposing a saboteur," said Tesla.

"And saving this movie!" added DeMarco.

His aunt put her face in her hands.

"Oh, DeMarco," she groaned.

"I'm sorry, kids, but you need to run along home," Cash Ashkinos said. "It might not look like it, but the grown-ups are trying to get some work done here."

The Veranda was an old theater—so old that it didn't have only a screen. It had a stage, too. Tesla jogged over and climbed the short flight of stairs and walked onstage. Nick and the other boys followed after her.

"I'm sorry, Mr. Ashkinos," Tesla said. "We're not leaving until we've told you what we know."

Bob Ortmann rolled his eyes and sighed. Then he turned to speak to the camera crew seated a few rows behind him.

"Go get someone from security, will ya?"

"Sure thing, Mr. Ortmann," someone said. The man who spoke popped from his seat and began making his way toward the aisle.

"As long as you're waiting for security to come hustle us away," Tesla said, "you might as well listen to what we have to say."

"Not really," said Ortmann. He pulled a cell phone from his jacket. "You go ahead and talk if you want. Me, I'm calling the studio to tell them about our latest fiasco."

"Well," Cash Ashkinos said, "you kids sure do have a sense of drama, I'll give you that. And remember, Damon, they did help you during that prank today."

Damon Wilder had seated himself in the front row, too, on Aunt Zoe's right, with several empty seats between them. Jack Wiltrout was in the seat next to Wilder; he was munching on yet another bag of chips. "That was no mere prank!" Wilder shouted, as if making sure that even the projectionist in the booth could hear him. "It was vicious sabotage! And *somebody* is going to suffer the consequences." He glared at Cash Ashkinos and Aunt Zoe.

Ashkinos stared back for a moment and then turned to Aunt Zoe. She looked too mortified to speak. "All right," Ashkinos continued. "If you kids want to continue your performance, go ahead. At least until your escort arrives. And then you go home quietly, deal?"

"Deal," Tesla said. "Ladies and gentlemen, my associates and I—"

"Associates?" DeMarco whispered.

"Partners!" Nick hissed.

Tesla glared at them. "All right. Ladies and gentlemen, my *partners* and I know who's been sabotaging this production. And we have proof!" She held our her hand to Nick, gesturing for him to hand her the script.

"Exhibit A!" Tesla waved the script over her head. Except that it wasn't the script. She realized that she was holding an empty soda bottle.

A snicker emanating from the audience sounded significantly like Damon Wilder's voice. It was followed by a few chuckles here and there.

"I'm sorry," Nick said. "I was going to recycle it. It shouldn't have been thrown in the trash." He took the bottle from Tesla and handed her the script.

"This," Tesla said, her voice echoing through the old theater, "is a script that Damon Wilder and Jack Wiltrout have been working on."

She stepped forward and tossed it down to Aunt Zoe in the front row.

"Wait—what? How did you get that?" Wilder demanded.

"It was found in a Dumpster earlier today," Nick said, his voice not quite as loud as Tesla's but loud enough. "I wanted in on the act," he whispered to his sister.

"You went through my trash?" Wilder sputtered.

"Yeah," Wiltrout said, "you went through . . . ?" He paused for a moment. "Wait a minute. Damon, you threw out our script?"

"Look, Jack, it was just the third draft, and we agreed that substantial rewrites were needed, remember?"

"Points for emoting, kids," Ashkinos said, "but your plotting needs work. We all know that Damon and Jack have been working on their own dialogue for *Metalman*."

"Their own *terrible* dialogue, you mean," said Silas.

Ashkinos winced and stole a quick peek toward a livid Wilder. "I didn't say that. My point was just that it doesn't prove anything," he said.

Aunt Zoe handed him the script.

"This isn't a rewrite of *The Stupefying Metalman*, Cash," she said.

He looked down at the ream of paper in his hands.

"*Reflections of Remembrance*," he read aloud. "A Play in Three Acts by Jack Wiltrout." Ashkinos looked up again at the kids on the stage in front of him. "I am very confused."

"Me, too," said Ortmann. By this time, he had lowered his phone and leaned forward to look over Ashkinos's shoulder at the script. Then he turned to his star and said, "Damon, you told me that you wanted Jack on set to punch up your dialogue. The studio is picking up the tab for that, not for you two to play Shakespeare."

"Oh, now, really—that's a bit insulting, Bob."

"Sure it is," he snapped. "It's insulting to Shakespeare!"

"Now, Bob," Jack said, after swallowing a mouthful of chips. "I assure you, I've been keeping my work on our play separate from my time on the *Metalman* script. I can account for all of my billable hours . . ."

"Excuse me, gentlemen," Aunt Zoe interrupted. She had taken the script from Cash and had been reading through it the whole time. She now rolled it up and pointed it at Wilder like a weapon. "Damon, Jack. When were you going to produce this play you were writing?"

The two men looked at her quizzically, as if they didn't understand the question.

Aunt Zoe looked directly at Tesla, and then she looked back at Damon Wilder and Jack Wiltrout.

"She knows," Tesla whispered to her friends. "She figured it out!"

"My aunt is no dummy," DeMarco said proudly.

"Hey," Silas whispered, "that reminds me. When are we going to get Michael back? We need that costume to finish *Bald Eagle*—"

"Silas!" Tesla hissed.

"I'm also wondering," Aunt Zoe continued, "where you were going to get the money to do it?"

With those words, a hush fell over the theater. The mumblings and chucklings and whisperings that had been heard in the background ceased as each person leaned forward to see what would happen next.

Wilder barked out an incredulous laugh. He answered in his loudest stage voice yet. "Where would we get the money? *I'm Damon Wilder!* I'm about to star in the biggest blockbuster of next year! After it comes out, I'll have theatrical producers fighting for the chance to finance any play I choose to do!"

DeMarco moved forward to stand beside Tesla.

"You've seen the performance he's turning in, Mr. Ortmann," DeMarco said. "Do you really think big-time Broadway producers are going to line up to pay him to be in a play?"

"Well . . ." Ortmann said.

"You wouldn't know about this, Bob," Ashkinos said, "but Zoe tells me that, earlier this summer, her nephew and his friends outsmarted two crooks who had kidnapped a little girl. And they got her home safe. Maybe they're on to something here."

Ortmann's eyes narrowed in concentration. "That would make a great feature," he said.

Now it was DeMarco's turn to look shocked. "You know about that?" he said to his aunt.

"Your mother has told me the story over and

over," Aunt Zoe said. "Don't tell her I said so, but she's proud of you."

Meanwhile, Damon Wilder's face had turned bright red. "That script doesn't prove anything," he said. "Now, why don't we send these kids home, and we'll get back to work." He swiveled this way and that to face Matt Gore and Barbara and the other crew members scattered around the theater. "Am I right, people?"

But no one told him he was right.

"Just one more thing," Tesla said. She motioned for Silas to step forward and hold up the dented metal he had carried in.

"This is part of the costume that Mr. Wilder was wearing this afternoon," Nick said. "Right, Mr. Gore?"

"Uhhh." Matt stood up and leaned in for a better look. "Yeah, that's it, all right. I had to throw it out because it got damaged during the—uh, the Itch and Moan incident." A groan rose throughout the theater. Matt shrugged. "Well, that's what they've been calling it on the Internet."

"If you look closely," Tesla said, "some of the powder is still inside."

"No! Don't go near it!" Wilder said.

DeMarco took a piece of the costume, the left shoulder plate, and walked to the front of the stage. He held the piece with its curved surface facing up like a bowl of soup. "It doesn't make you itch," he said. "I already tested it. But come and get a closer look." He kneeled at the edge of the stage; Aunt Zoe and Cash walked over and took the piece from DeMarco's hands. They held it up and peered at it closely.

"Looks like some sort of crumbs," Cash said.

"What's that smell?" Aunt Zoe said, sniffing cautiously at first and then taking a good long whiff. "Smells like, like . . ."

"Corn chips!" Cash Ashkinos shouted.

"Correct," Tesla said. "Corn chips. Isn't that right, Mr. Wiltrout?"

A murmur rippled through the old theater. All eyes turned toward Jack Wiltrout, who had jumped up from his seat. He opened his mouth to speak but found that he could not.

His mouth was full of corn chips.

He let the bag drop from his hand. "Nm hmm mmm hmm hmmm," he mumbled. And then, after a few mighty chews that cleared his mouth, he said,

"Now wait just a minute—"

Nick cleared his throat. "There was no itching powder. Just crumbs planted inside the costume. And that leaked video of Mr. Wilder's conveniently timed temper tantrum didn't come from a spy. It came from an accomplice who knew exactly when and where Mr. Wilder was going to make a scene."

Just in case anyone couldn't tell who was being accused, Nick threw a significant look in the direction of Jack Wiltrout, erasing any doubt.

"This is insane!" Wiltrout protested.

"Oh, come on!" Wilder cried. "Why would I put Fritos in my costume? Why would I want to humiliate myself on the Internet?"

"Why would you start behaving like a loon?" Ortmann added. "Why would you suddenly lose all your skill as an actor? Why would you antagonize two of the smartest, most talented, most professional people I've ever worked with?"

"Three words answer all those questions," Aunt Zoe said. She turned toward the stage. "Tesla?"

"Pay or play," Tesla said.

Zoe started nodding. And then Cash Ashkinos started nodding. Then Bob Ortmann and Matt Gore and Barbara the makeup lady started nodding. The camera crew, the P.A.s, everyone in the theater, everyone working on *The Stupefying Metalman*—they all knew those three words and why they explained everything.

"You get paid even if you're fired," Tesla said. "And if you're fired, and you're paid the millions you'd be owed, then you'd have the time *and* the money to go off and do your own play."

"So you acted like a jerk and leaked your horrible performance and wrote yourself awful dialogue and pretended that you wanted Aunt Zoe and Mr. Ashkinos fired," Nick said. "All because what you really wanted was for the studio to fire you."

A startled silence fell over the crowd.

"Have you all lost your minds?" Wiltrout said incredulously. "You're actually listening to this drivel? Where is security? I mean, this is nuts! Right, Damon? Right?"

When Wiltrout realized that his colleague wasn't going to back him up, his face turned pale. "Oh, no," he said. "Damon, don't do it, man!"

But it was too late. Wiltrout knew what was coming. He knew that Wilder was an actor through and through. Which meant that he couldn't pass up the chance to perform a time-honored role: that of the criminal caught in the act, one who must make a dramatic, scene-chewing, over-the-top confession.

"Yes! All right! I admit it!" Wilder proclaimed. "I never wanted to do this stupid movie! Do you know why I got the part? Because I look like the guy in the comic book! That's it! That's all it took! If my agent weren't so good, I would've gotten chump change that I could walk away from. But five million bucks? Pay or play? How could I say no? But the second I put on that dumb costume, I knew I couldn't go through with it. I almost went to Juilliard! I played Laertes at the Hudson Valley Shakespeare Festival! The *New York Times* named me Off-Off-Off-Broadway's second-most promising male talent under thirty, two years in a row! I starred in three films shot entirely in black and white, and I made the cover of *Indie Cred* magazine. Twice! And what happens to me? A guest spot doing flying broomstick gags on *The Witches of Greenwich Village* followed by the chance to play the world's lamest superhero. I mean, give me a break! Metalman? We all know he's just an Iron Man rip-off, with a little Silver Surfer thrown in."

"All right, Damon, that's enough," Cash Ashkinos said.

But Wilder wasn't done. "And the script really *is* terrible!" he said. "No matter how good I might have been in this movie, it would have ruined me for the serious stage. So the only thing to do was *not* to be in it, but still get the money I needed to make my dream come true."

"Damon," Ashkinos said, his voice sharper now. "Enough."

"You really should stop talking," Wiltrout said gently. He threw a look at the audience watching intently from their seats. "Witnesses, man. And later—lawyers."

Wilder crossed his arms. "Damon Wilder has said his piece."

"What's going on?" someone called out from back of the room. "I heard there was trouble."

It was Dalasia, the security guard.

"No trouble. Everything's under control . . . now," Ortmann called back. "Still, just to be safe, why don't you escort Mr. Wilder and Mr. Wiltrout from the set?"

Looking confused but resolute, Dalasia came

down the aisle toward the men. They left with her without resisting. Ortmann trailed after them. "I've gotta call the studio!" he said, pulling out his cell phone and frantically hitting the numbers.

"Lucky for us it took so long for security to get here," DeMarco said.

"Maybe not luck," Tesla said, tilting her head toward the back of the theater. "There's the guy who went to get the security guard." It was their friend the Teamster. He was grinning, and then he raised his hands and gave the kids two thumbs-up.

As Wilder and Wiltrout were escorted out, a pair of hands slapped together. Then another. And then another. The rhythm of the clapping was slow at first, but it grew faster and louder as it spread throughout the theater.

Aunt Zoe and Cash Ashkinos and Matt Gore and the others weren't applauding the exit of their (soon-to-be former) star, though.

They were applauding the four young people who had just put on the greatest performance any of them had ever seen.

Uncle Newt and his kinda-sorta girlfriend, Hiroko, were in the dining room when Nick and Tesla finally got home.

Hiroko was seated at the dining room table. Uncle Newt was hanging over it.

Apparently, Uncle Newt had decided (as he did from time to time) to eat "astronaut style." That is, suspended from the ceiling via a harness and straps.

"Hey, kids!" he said. "How was your day?"

"Fine," grunted Tesla.

"Okay," grunted Nick.

"Did you get to visit that movie set like you'd hoped?" asked Hiroko.

"Yeah," grunted Tesla.

"Umm-hmm," grunted Nick.

"And how was it?" said Uncle Newt.

"Fine," grunted Tesla.

"Okay," grunted Nick.

They usually weren't so impolite, but it really had been a *looong* day.

"Well, we'll have dinner in about an hour, as soon as I finish my snack and do some tests down in the lab. You can tell us all about it over some yummy bread and water," Uncle Newt said.

"And macaroni and asparagus," Hiroko added.

"Oh, yeah," Uncle Newt added. "And some stuff Hiroko brought over."

"Sound good?"

"Yeah," grunted Tesla.

"Umm-hmm," grunted Nick.

Then they trudged up the stairs, separating when they reached the top. Tesla heading to the bathroom, Nick to the bedroom.

Tesla knew exactly what her brother was going to do. The Stoplite program must have turned itself off by now, which meant that Nick could finally turn on the laptop and get back to his cyber-sleuthing. Tesla reached for the soap.

"Tez! Come here! Quick!" Nick called out frantically.

Tesla spun on her heel and ran down the hall. She skidded to a stop in the doorway of the bedroom she shared with her brother.

There was Nick, sitting on the floor, hunched over the laptop, just as she had expected.

What she hadn't expected—what she couldn't have anticipated—was the message she saw flashing on the screen:

> OPEN THIS FILE IF YOU WANT
> TO SAVE YOUR PARENTS....
>
> OPEN THIS FILE IF YOU WANT
> TO SAVE YOUR PARENTS....
>
> OPEN THIS FILE IF YOU WANT
> TO SAVE YOUR PARENTS....

Nick reached for the keyboard.

"Wait," said Tesla. "We don't know who sent that or what it is. It could be spam, or it could have a virus, or it could be some kind of trick . . ."

"Why would a spammer send *that* message? And if we don't read it, we'll never know if it's a trick or not."

"Okay, but let's at least get Uncle Newt to look at it. He must have some scanning software that can check it out—"

"Tez! I'm the cautious one, remember? And I say we open it." Nick reached for the keyboard as Tesla lunged to pull the laptop away. His finger poked at the Enter key . . .

And then there was a muffled boom.

And the whole house seemed to lift about a half inch before slamming down again.

And the lights flickered.

And then everything went black. Including the laptop screen.

From somewhere downstairs, Uncle Newt's voice rang out:

"I'm all right!" he shouted, followed by, "It's a surprise!"

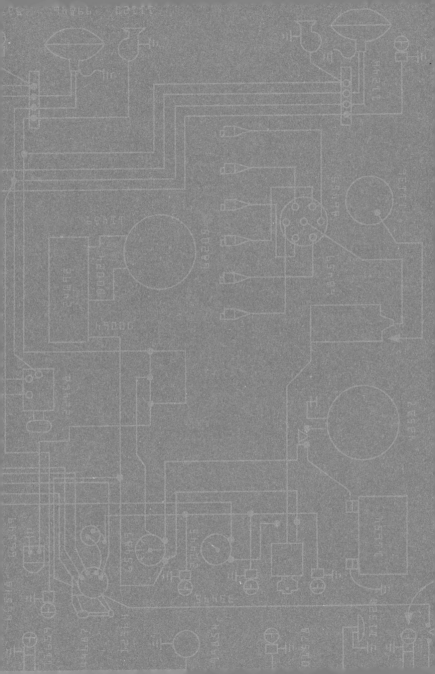

Collect all of the electrifying
Nick and Tesla
adventures!

**Nick and Tesla's
High-Voltage Danger Lab**

**Nick and Tesla's
Robot Army Rampage**

**Nick and Tesla's
Secret Agent Gadget Battle**

**Nick and Tesla's
Super-Cyborg Gadget Glove**

**Visit NickandTesla.com for updates,
instructions, photos, and more!**

NICK AND TESLA'S

HIGH-VOLTAGE DANGER LAB

A MYSTERY WITH ELECTROMAGNETS, BURGLAR ALARMS, AND OTHER GADGETS YOU CAN BUILD YOURSELF

BY "SCIENCE BOB" PFLUGFELDER AND STEVE HOCKENSMITH

NICK AND TESLA'S

ROBOT ARMY RAMPAGE

A MYSTERY WITH HOVERBOTS, BRISTLEBOTS, AND OTHER ROBOTS YOU CAN BUILD YOURSELF

BY "SCIENCE BOB" PFLUGFELDER AND STEVE HOCKENSMITH

NICK AND TESLA'S

SECRET AGENT GADGET BATTLE

A MYSTERY WITH SPY CAMERAS, CODE WHEELS, AND OTHER GADGETS YOU CAN BUILD YOURSELF

BY "SCIENCE BOB" PFLUGFELDER AND STEVE HOCKENSMITH

NICK AND TESLA'S

SUPER-CYBORG GADGET GLOVE

A MYSTERY WITH A BLINKING, BEEPING, VOICE-RECORDING GADGET GLOVE YOU CAN BUILD YOURSELF

BY "SCIENCE BOB" PFLUGFELDER AND STEVE HOCKENSMITH

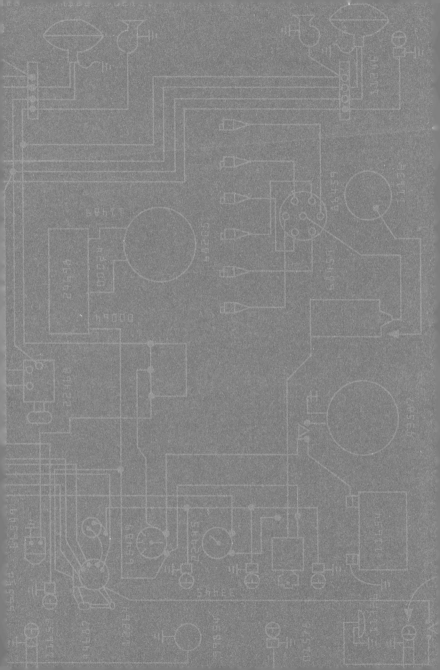

About the Authors

"SCIENCE BOB" PFLUGFELDER is an award-winning elementary school science teacher. His fun and informative approach to science has led to television appearances on the History Channel and *Access Hollywood*. He is also a regular guest on *Jimmy Kimmel Live*, *The Dr. Oz Show*, and *Live with Kelly & Michael*. Articles on Bob's experiments have appeared in *People*, *Nickelodeon* magazine, *Popular Science*, *Disney's Family Fun*, and *Wired*. He lives in Watertown, Massachusetts.

STEVE HOCKENSMITH is the author of the Edgar-nominated Holmes on the Range mystery series. His other books include the New York Times best seller *Pride and Prejudice and Zombies: Dawn of the Dreadfuls* and the short-story collection *Naughty: Nine Tales of Christmas Crime*. He lives with his wife and two children about forty minutes from Half Moon Bay, California.